**Christopher leaned close enough that Ashley could feel his breath on her cheek. "Stay here."**

"Where are you going?" She grabbed his arm, desperate to keep her only known ally close—even if he had broken her heart at one time.

He locked gazes with her, that same confidence that had always made her feel safe shining in his gaze. "I'm going to find something to fight with."

"But they have guns!"

"If I go down, I'm going to go down fighting, Ashley." His voice was steady, holding not even a hint of disbelief. "I want you to stay in here. Understand?"

He tried to stand but Ashley pulled him back down. "I came here for your help, not to get you killed."

His eyes softened for a moment. "I know. Trust me. Okay?"

She didn't know if she could ever trust him again. But, in this moment, she had no choice. She nodded. Her heart pounded in her ears as he pulled the door open.

Something creaked outside.

The steps. Someone was coming up the steps.

Fear squeezed tighter as she braced herself for whatever was about to come.

**Books by Christy Barritt**

Love Inspired Suspense

*Keeping Guard*
*The Last Target*
*Race Against Time*
*Ricochet*
\*Key Witness
\*Lifeline
\*High-Stakes Holiday Reunion

*The Security Experts

## *CHRISTY BARRITT*

loves stories and has been writing them for as long as she can remember. She gets her best ideas when she's supposed to be paying attention to something else—like in a workshop or while driving down the road.

The second book in her Squeaky Clean Mystery series, *Suspicious Minds,* won the inspirational category of the 2009 Daphne du Maurier Award for Excellence in Suspense and Mystery. She's also the coauthor of *Changed: True Stories of Finding God in Christian Music.*

When she's not working on books, Christy writes articles for various publications. She's also a weekly feature writer for the *Virginian-Pilot* newspaper, the worship leader at her church and a frequent speaker at various writers' groups, women's luncheons and church events.

She's married to Scott, a teacher and funny man extraordinaire. They have two sons, two dogs and a houseplant named Martha.

To learn more about her, visit her website, www.christybarritt.com.

# HIGH-STAKES
# HOLIDAY REUNION

## CHRISTY BARRITT

PAPL
DISCARDED

**HARLEQUIN**® LOVE INSPIRED® SUSPENSE

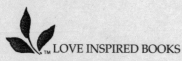

LOVE INSPIRED BOOKS

Recycling programs for this product may not exist in your area.

ISBN-13: 978-0-373-44563-9

HIGH-STAKES HOLIDAY REUNION

www.Harlequin.com

**Printed in U.S.A.**

Peace I leave with you; my peace I give to you.
Not as the world gives do I give to you. Let not your
hearts be troubled, neither let them be afraid.
—*John* 14:27

This book is dedicated to my readers.
Your friendship and notes of encouragement
mean the world to me and always brighten my day.

# ONE

As Ashley Wilson rounded the corner, her foot slammed onto the brakes.

What…?

In the distance, her brother's house came into view. A commotion on the lawn caused her blood to freeze.

Three men in suits scuffled near the sidewalk. Her brother Josh's tall, lanky form jerked in the middle of the crowd as he struggled against the men. What were they doing to her brother? Who were these men?

Her gaze went to the two black sedans parked at the curb. The men were trying to…force her brother into one?

She yanked her gaze from the scene to her clock. David. Where was the eight-year-old? His bus hadn't come yet. It couldn't have. Ashley was on her way to meet him, but had arrived a good ten minutes early.

Still, panic raced through her.

She wanted to throw the car into Park, rush from her seat and intercede. But there was no way she could over-take all of those men.

Her gaze zoomed in on the black metal at one of the men's waistband. A gun. These men were armed.

Her heart stopped when she saw a tiny head bobbing in the crowd.

David. Her precious nephew, David. Her reason for waking up in the morning. Her reason for working at home as a web designer with flexible hours. Her heartbeat.

They had David. She covered her mouth as a guttural cry escaped.

How had they gotten David? He was supposed to be in school. Had Josh pulled him out early today?

Some of her logic returned, hitting her with the force of a lightning bolt. The police. She had to call the police. That was all there was to it.

She reached into her purse and fumbled with the cell phone, her hands trembling so badly she wasn't sure she could dial.

She glanced up just in time to see one of the men point her way and yell something.

Two of the men pulled their guns and began running toward her car.

Toward her.

She threw the car in Reverse. She had to get away. If they caught her then there'd be no way she could help. She slammed her foot onto the accelerator. Her neck snapped back with the force, but she didn't care. Adrenaline pumped through her veins.

That's when she heard the first pop. Her heart sped. They were shooting at her. She ducked just as the windshield shattered.

She screamed but kept going. Reaching the street behind her, she pulled hard on the steering wheel, threw the car into Drive and squealed off. Another pop sounded behind her but didn't reach her car.

She glanced in her rearview mirror. The men had stopped running. She'd lost them. For now.

She craned her neck, trying to see beyond the eerie, spiderweb-like lines etched into her windshield. She could hardly see the road. Finally, she reached the street leading away from the neighborhood.

Her mind raced a million miles a minute. What had just happened? What should she do now?

The police, she remembered. She needed to call the police.

Grief crushed her heart. David. Poor David. She needed to help him, to soothe him and wipe his tears. Since Josh's wife had died, Ashley had filled in as a mother figure. Now her heart squeezed with a maternal grief.

No, the best thing she could do was to let the authorities know. There was no way her 120 pounds could take down all three of those men. Probably not even one of them.

Keeping one eye on the road, she grabbed the phone, which had fallen to the floor in her haste to escape. Her fingers trembled on the keypad. Before she could dial, the phone beeped with an incoming call.

She saw the number, and her heart raced—first with hope, then dread. Her brother?

She looked back at the road, swerving away from an oncoming car. Quickly, she answered. "Josh? What's going on?"

"You can't call the police, Ashley." His words tumbled into each other, and panic laced his voice, making its pitch rise.

"Josh, I'm scared."

"Ashley—"

Before he could finish, another voice came on the line. "We'll find you and kill you, Ashley Wilson. You weren't supposed to see that."

The words sent cold fear through her. "Who is this? What do you want with my brother?"

"Stay out of it," the man growled.

Even the sound of his voice conjured up images of evil,

of a heartless man. "What about David? Can I just get David? Leave him out of this. Please. He's just a child."

Suddenly, the black sedan appeared in her rearview mirror—coming fast and closing the space between them too quickly. Memories of her accident began to crush her last shred of sanity. No, she couldn't let her mind go there. Not now.

She swerved onto a side road, the phone slipping from her hand as she gripped the wheel. She didn't have time to worry about it now. She accelerated. A glance behind her confirmed that the car turned down the same street. A man hung out the side window, a gun in hand.

She had to think, and quickly. She didn't have much time.

Just then, the back glass shattered. She screamed, trying to maintain her control of the car. Wind—cold and sharp—whipped around her. Pellets of glass rained down from her hair. She couldn't drive like this much longer. It wasn't safe—for her or anyone around her.

But her survival instinct was greater than her fear. She had to stay alive—not for her sake, but for David's.

A busy highway waited ahead. Before she reached it, she turned onto another side street. Immediately, she pulled into a parking lot. A shopping center shadowed her car as she drove full-speed in front of the structure. At the corner, she swerved around the building and slammed on the brakes.

Maybe they hadn't seen her. Hopefully, they'd assumed that she'd gone straight.

But just in case they didn't, she grabbed her purse and her phone and jumped out of the car.

Two delivery trucks were parked behind the strip mall, and their drivers were unloading boxes of product. Ashley picked the closest one and ran toward him. He looked up as she approached, his eyebrows furrowed in curiosity.

"I'm sorry," she mumbled, not stopping to ask permission. She ran through the propped-open door instead, darted through the back offices and break room and into a hardware store.

Her gaze fluttered wildly about the building. Where now? Where could she hide?

The black sedan flew past the front windows of the store. They knew she'd come this way. Now what did she do?

She crouched down, waiting until the car disappeared.

Then she sprinted out the front door and toward the opposite end of the row of shops. What store had that other delivery truck been stopped behind? She pictured the design on the truck. Pastries.

Taking a guess, she slipped inside a drug store, running until she reached the back.

"Hey, what are you doing?" A man in a cashier's smock held up a hand to stop her as she charged into the door marked "Employees Only."

"Sorry." She didn't stop to hear his response. She went straight to the back door. She paused there, slowly peeking around the edge of it.

She spotted the black sedan parked haphazardly beside her car. A man jumped from the vehicle and ran in through that same delivery door and into the hardware store. It was only a matter of moments before they found her and killed her. She couldn't let that happen.

The other delivery truck wasn't far away. Only a few feet. The driver had packed up and was climbing into the front. That truck seemed her only hope at the moment.

She crept outside, concealed behind a Dumpster. If she ran, she might make it onto the back of the truck before the driver realized what was happening. She had to. It was her only chance.

Staying low, she slunk toward the truck. The engine started. She didn't have much time. If she was going to make a move, it had to be now.

*Lord, help me.*

She lunged toward the back door. Her hand connected with the handle.

It opened. Praise God, it opened.

She swung into the back of the truck, colliding with a rack full of prepackaged donuts and cupcakes. She closed the door just as the man in black exited the hardware store.

She was going to get away, she realized.

But her heartbeat didn't slow as she wondered if her brother and nephew would be so fortunate.

Christopher Jordan ran a hand over his face, weariness from a long, hard week of work compounding until a pulsing headache thumped at the back of his head. He'd worked too late—again. Now darkness surrounded his car as he drove the hour back to his house.

He really should buy a place closer to work. But this house had lots of memories for him, and he couldn't give those up yet. He needed those memories now. He needed good memories to push out all of the bad ones.

He turned off the highway, and the streets became quieter, darker. Just like his soul, he thought. Ever since he returned from war, he hadn't felt like himself.

Just how was he going to remedy that?

Good memories, he thought. He just needed to hold on to the good. That, along with his faith in God, would help to pull him through his inner turmoil.

Finally, he turned onto his street. All he could think about was getting home for the weekend, being alone and not doing anything for as long as humanly possible—which meant until Monday came and it was back to work again.

He knew his stress was from more than just his work. He'd only been back from the Middle East for three months, and memories of the place still haunted him. Every night, nightmares jolted him awake. Too many images stained his mind. It seemed as if they'd been imprinted on his soul, and for the rest of his life he'd carry the burden of his time deployed.

He'd gotten out of the military, taken a job as a training specialist at the private security contracting firm Iron, Incorporated, also known as Eyes. He taught tactical training, such as sharpshooting and use of force to law-enforcement groups that came to Eyes for instruction. Eyes worked with both local law-enforcement communities, as well as the Department of Defense, in training personnel, developing programs and equipment, and for other special assignments.

He'd taken the job in hopes of repairing some of the damage his psyche had suffered. He'd thought he was stronger than all of this. But the deaths of those around him had begun to take their toll on him, and now he wondered if he'd ever be the same.

He'd poured himself into work at his new job, hoping to erase the pain. But it was always there, cold and achy and throbbing.

The two-story house that his grandfather had left to him came into view. The place was out in the middle of nowhere. Some would call it isolated. Christopher called it breathing room. He slowed as he turned into his driveway, his headlights skimming the front of the house.

His foot pressed on the brakes. Was that something on his porch? In his rocking chair?

In the dark, he could hardly tell. Something was out of place, but whatever was on the rocking chair only appeared to be a shadow.

He should have left the porch light on, he supposed, but he hadn't thought about it when he left home this morning. Now all of his instincts were on alert. Could it have to do with his SEAL team bringing down the leader of that terrorist group? Had their names been leaked? They'd all be logical targets in the aftermath of the terrorist group's demise.

But especially Christopher. He'd been the one to pull the trigger.

He reached under the front seat and pulled out the gun he kept there. He carried it with him at all times as a part of his job.

Slowly, cautiously, he got out of his car. Yes, there was definitely something on his porch. Or was it…someone?

He crept toward the steps. The bitter cold air filled his lungs, heightening his awareness even more. Who would be hanging out on his porch at night? Had one of the terrorists found him?

With his other hand, he fingered the phone in his pocket. Should he call for backup? No, not yet. They'd only think he was paranoid, only push him harder to get more counseling for PTSD. The last thing this soldier wanted to do was talk about his feelings, especially with a stranger.

He scanned the usually welcoming porch again. The railing still looked intact. Even the strands of evergreen that he'd draped there, complete with red Christmas bows, were in place. He didn't see anyone lurking behind the bushes or peeking around the corner of the house.

With the skill of a trained fighter, he climbed the steps, his gun pointed at the figure on his porch. He couldn't see a face. The person appeared to be hiding underneath a coat—arms, legs, face and all.

He cocked his gun, all of his instincts on alert, each of his muscles poised for action. "You have three seconds to show yourself before I fire."

The figure flinched, and a mad fluttering of limbs ensued. Finally, a head popped up. Familiar eyes stared at him, wide with fear. The facts hit him one by one. Honey-blond hair. Oval face. Slim build. He couldn't see the color of her eyes, but he instinctively knew they were blue.

The woman raised a slender hand. "Please, don't shoot. It's me." Her voice sounded soft, lyrical—and desperate.

"Ashley?" He lowered his gun, disbelief washing over him. It couldn't be. No, not Ashley. Not his ex-fiancée, the woman whose heart he'd broken when he'd called off their engagement. Their parting had been one of the most painful conversations he'd ever had, and still when he thought about it today, an ache formed in his chest. He'd had to make a decision between his career or a family. His country had needed him, so he'd chosen his career. He tried to live without regret; he thought he was stronger than that. But whenever he allowed himself to think about Ashley, regret was the very emotion that tried to creep into his mind. He'd loved that woman at one time. Times had changed, though; he had changed.

She nodded slowly, raw emotion lining her eyes. She pulled the white, wool coat around her more tightly as the wind picked up again, sweeping dry leaves across the porch. The sound tightened his nerves.

"Christopher."

Instinctively, he stepped closer. He'd both dreamed and had nightmares about this moment for so long. During those dark moments on the battlefield, he'd wondered what it would be like to see Ashley again.

And never had he imagined it like this. Not him with a gun in his hand and her with a look of absolute vulnerability straining each of her lovely features. No, in his moments when he'd faced death, he'd imagined Ashley forgiving him, smiling, picking up where they'd left off. He knew that would never happen. Even if there weren't any hard feelings between them, Christopher knew he was too broken and damaged to be in a relationship right now.

He remembered their last conversation and paused, unsure how to greet her. Not with a hug. Not with the way things had ended. A handshake seemed too formal when considering their past relationship. Instead, he settled for putting his gun away and making an effort to relax his shoulders.

He and Ashley had met at a mutual friend's house on New Year's Eve more than a decade ago, and it had been a textbook case of love at first sight. Not only had he instantly thought she was beautiful, but her smile, her love for life, her hope for the future had hooked him. She'd pulled him out of the shell he easily sucked himself into—most people didn't see it because he'd hidden it well with easygoing small talk. But Ashley had always seen right through him. She had a way about her that made him open up.

Their two years together were filled with easy, effortless moments. Relationships like that didn't happen often. Six months before the wedding, he'd called things off.

Ashley brushed a hair out of her face and licked her lips. Her eyes implored him. "I'm sorry to show up here, but I didn't know where else to go." Her voice sounded tight and strained.

He reached toward her, compassion and concern pounding through his veins, but his hand dropped midway. "Are you okay?"

She hesitated and then shook her head. Those wide, pleading eyes met his again. "I need your help."

He stared at her another moment, thoughts and emotions colliding inside him. His help? What could he possibly help her with? Whatever it was, his gut told him it was serious. "Let's go inside. Get you out of the cold."

As she stepped closer, Christopher wanted to soak her in, to absorb all the changes in her over the past several years. But he couldn't do that. It was no longer his right.

He unlocked the door, noticing that she was shivering uncontrollably. From the cold? Or from something deeper?

He flipped the light on in the entryway and dust bunnies floated across the wooden floor. Perhaps he'd neglected housekeeping more than he should have. He offered an apologetic grin. "I wasn't expecting to see you. I would have straightened up some."

She stepped inside, her face grim with…sorrow? Fear? Grief? His grin slipped. With a hand on her back, he led her into the living room where boxes still waited along the walls for him to unpack.

She shivered again. "Believe me. I wasn't expecting to be here. I only came here because I was desperate."

The brutal honesty of her words stung. She'd made it clear when they last talked that she never wanted to see him again. Christopher couldn't blame her. Things had ended badly. He'd made the best decision possible at the time. But in hindsight, he'd wondered if it was the worst decision ever.

He didn't have time to think about what could have been now. Instead, he led her to the couch, one that had been left here by his grandfather. This was probably the same sofa that had been here back when he and Ashley were dating, when they used to come over and play dominoes with his granddad. "Have a seat."

She lowered herself and folded her arms across her chest. Her legs were crossed at the ankles, and trembles still claimed her muscles. Her gaze pulled on his. "I'm in trouble, Christopher. I didn't know where else to go."

His jaw flexed under the weight of her words, but he nodded. "Go on."

"My brother and nephew have been kidnapped, and you're the only one who can help."

# TWO

Ashley swallowed hard as she watched Christopher blink and tilt his head. It would take anyone some time to comprehend her words. She was still having a hard time comprehending them.

"Say that again?" His voice held a touch of disbelief and confusion.

She shook her head, emotion tightening her muscles. "Listen, I know it's a lot to take in. I'm still trying to take it all in. It just seems like a nightmare, but it's not." She closed her eyes, wishing this was all just a bad dream and that she'd wake up to find everyone safe and sound. Things like this didn't happen to ordinary people like Ashley. Only it *had* happened.

Christopher shifted in his seat and leaned toward her, his full attention on her. He'd always been such a good listener. At one time, it had been one of the many qualities she'd loved about him. Their breakup had devastated her, though. Now almost every memory of him caused hurt instead of joy. Those hurts had been compounding for nearly a decade. Only desperation would lead her back here.

"Why don't you start from the beginning?" Christopher urged.

She sucked in a deep breath before recounting the story,

detail by detail. Christopher listened quietly, nodding on occasion. He murmured words of encouragement as he tried to grasp her story.

"You jumped on the back of a bakery truck to escape?" He squinted.

She nodded, knowing how crazy she sounded. It was amazing the things a person did while fighting to survive. She'd been there before—emotionally, at least. "I jumped off at the next stop."

"And how'd you end up here?"

"I ran into Karina about a month ago at the grocery store, and she told me that you were back in town." Karina was married to a SEAL and remained a distant but mutual friend. "I used my cell phone to find Karina's number and asked if she knew where you were living now. She said at your granddad's old place. I snuck off the truck, called a taxi and now I'm here."

He stared at her a moment, an unreadable expression on his face. "Ashley, if you don't mind me asking, why here? Why me?"

How could she tell him the truth about how Josh and David's disappearance affected him also? She couldn't. Not yet. She'd only tell him the secret she'd been carrying with her for years as a last, desperate measure.

For so long, she'd been bitter about Christopher walking out of her life. Now here she was, basically at his mercy. Where did she even start?

She held her hands in the air to show her confusion. The action also showed her surrender. She'd basically raised her white flag when she arrived here, an unspoken agreement to put the past behind them. But could she really do that? She let out her breath slowly. "I don't know where else to go. I can't go to the police. I think these men would kill Josh and David if I did." She glanced at her hands, now in her lap. "I thought maybe you could help."

Christopher leaned forward. He'd aged since Ashley had last seen him. He used to have the boy-next-door look about him. He'd been all-American with his tousled blond hair, easy smile and friendly green eyes. What had changed besides the fact that he was beefier now, more man and less boy? He was still chiseled and defined. He carried himself with his head raised high and his eyes wide and alert. He was confident, capable and tough.

But right now, whenever he looked at her, a strange emotion loomed in the depths of his eyes. Weariness? Hardness? Apathy? She didn't know.

"Why would someone abduct your brother and his little boy, Ashley? That's what doesn't make any sense to me."

She shook her head, grief clutching her heart again as their parting images filled her mind. "I don't know. Josh had been working on some big projects for his company. He never told me any details, though, as to what exactly he was doing."

He shifted but kept his gaze on her. "He's some kind of computer genius, right?"

She nodded. "He's absolutely brilliant when it comes to anything to do with technology. There's nothing he can't do."

He rubbed his hands on his jeans and shook his head. "How about his wife? Have you talked to her? Does she know about any of this?"

"She died three years ago. Cancer." Her heart panged as she said the words aloud.

"I'm sorry, Ashley. You said they had a son? I knew they'd been trying."

Ashley's throat burned as she nodded. She remembered all of the Sunday brunches Christopher had shared with her family. He'd seemed to fit right in. That part of her life seemed so long ago. So much had changed since then. "David. He's eight, and he's a wonderful little boy." Her voice caught. "I'm so worried about him, Christopher."

Christopher stood and ran a hand over his face. "I'm not an expert at tracking down missing persons, Ashley. Terrorists, maybe. But this…I want to help. I really do. I just…"

"Please, Christopher. I don't know where else to go." She looked up at him, hoping her eyes conveyed her desperation. She would have never come to him unless she was desperate. He had to know that.

He was silent a moment before nodding. "Let me call some of my friends at Eyes. Maybe they can—"

"Eyes?"

He nodded. "They're a private security contracting firm."

"I've heard murmurs about them in the area. I didn't realize you worked for them now. Karina just said that you were a contractor for the Department of Defense."

"That's right. I'm a training specialist. It's a nice change from what I was doing. I'm sure someone there can help us. The men who run the operation have connections… well, everywhere. Local law enforcement, FBI, CIA, you name it."

"That sounds perfect. Thank you." A touch of hope filled her for the first time since all of this had happened.

He pointed outside. "In the meantime, the apartment over the garage isn't much, but you can stay there tonight, if you want."

She shook her head harder than intended and started to rise. "I can't even think about sleeping. I need to go find them, Christopher. Now. Don't you understand?"

His hand covered her arm, and he pulled her back down

onto the sofa. "Ashley, I know you want to go out there and search, but we have no idea where to even look. We need a plan. We at least need a clue. If we go out there right now, all we'll be doing is driving around in circles. It's best if we get a good night's rest and start fresh tomorrow morning."

The truth of his words washed over her. It wasn't what she wanted to hear, but he did make sense. If they left tonight, where would they go? What exactly would they do? She had no idea.

Finally, she nodded. "You're right. I can call a taxi, though. Go to a hotel for the night."

"Don't be silly. You should stay close, just in case."

Just in case what? Her throat burned, but the question wouldn't leave her lips. Instead, she said, "Okay. I hate to impose, but I don't have a lot of choices right now."

Her cell phone buzzed in her pocket. She pulled it out and saw that she had a text message.

*Tell anyone and the boy dies*

She gasped and dropped the phone. They wouldn't really hurt little David, would they? She squeezed the skin between her eyes and began praying.

"What is it?" Christopher leaned down and picked up the phone. The words he read there made his blood go cold. He glanced up at Ashley and saw that her face was deathly pale. The woman looked as if she were on the brink of a breakdown. Who wouldn't be, in her shoes? Two of the people she loved most in the world had been snatched right in front of her, and she was sure to feel helpless about what to do.

A tear trickled down her face. She looked so alone

with her arms pulled across her chest. Christopher put her phone on the table and impulsively pulled her into his arms in a feeble attempt to offer comfort.

She stiffened in his embrace. Bad idea, he realized. Really bad idea.

He released her, his throat tight with emotion. "I'm sorry, Ashley."

She sighed. "I am, too."

The way she said the words made him wonder about their meaning. What was she sorry about? That he was the only one who could help her?

Her eyes met his, and he could see the emotions pulling at her.

"I didn't come back to rekindle a romance, Christopher," she whispered. "You know that. Right?"

He nodded, picking up on the compassion and sensitivity in her words. "Of course."

Part of him had never forgotten about Ashley, but he knew she wouldn't forgive him for calling off their engagement. It was just as well that way. At least their rift would help them both keep their distance.

He pointed toward the back door, ready to end this conversation. "How about if I show you upstairs?"

Maybe some time away from each other would be just what they both needed. Put them in the same room for ten minutes and fireworks had begun exploding—and not the good kind of fireworks, either.

He grabbed some sheets and blankets before they stepped out the back door. Darkness surrounded them. Christopher reached back inside to flip on a small light, but nothing happened. "Must be burned out," he muttered. "Just watch your step."

The full force of winter was evident in the dried leaves along the wooden floorboards beneath them and the skeletal outline of trees in the distance. The entire back side of the house faced the beautiful and massive James River. The grass faded into marshland and then into glimmering blue water—when you could see it during the daytime hours, at least. Tonight, all that was visible was the blackness.

"Follow me." Christopher led her up a flight of wooden stairs, pulled out some keys and unlocked the door just as another breeze swept over the area. "I heard we might get some snow," he muttered, pushing the door open. Their conversation somehow seemed awkward, like they were strangers trying to fill the silence.

"Yeah, I heard that, too. It's been a while since we've had a good snowstorm in this area." Her cheeks flushed as she said the words.

Christopher remembered a snowstorm they'd had here nine years ago. He and Ashley had spent the whole weekend huddled inside together by the fire and talking about forever. They'd talked about marriage and children and how they were going to celebrate their 25th anniversary. Too many memories for his comfort.

They stepped into the apartment, which was located over a detached garage. He tried the light switch, but again, nothing happened. "Must be a breaker. I'll check on it in a second. Let me just put these sheets down."

As he placed the sheets on the bed in the darkened room, his gaze scanned the place quickly. He'd only been up here once since he'd been back, but the place appeared untouched. He turned back toward Ashley, who stood uncomfortably in the center of the room, her arms wrapped around herself again. His gaze latched on to her a moment. Was it even possible that she was more beautiful than before? She'd filled out more, but the extra weight looked good on her. She looked more naturally beautiful with only a little makeup on and her hair straight and long—fuss-free, if he had to guess.

She looked up at him, the strain in her eyes obvious. "I know this is awkward, and I'm sorry about that. I'll repay you for your help. I don't know how, but I will."

How did Christopher tell her that he was the one who needed to repay her for all of the heartache he'd caused? He bit down on his lip. He couldn't.

All he could do was to help her find her brother and nephew.

As much as Ashley resented the man in front of her, God had been trying to teach her a lesson in forgiveness lately. Yet she'd kept holding on. Now she would have no choice but to face her feelings of resentment and abandonment head-on.

Christopher stepped closer, the raw look in his eyes making her throat go dry. She wondered what had changed in him over the past several years since she'd seen him last. "I'm glad you came to me, Ashley. I want to help."

*Nothing will ever make up for your choosing your career over me.* She didn't say the words aloud. Instead, she reached for the sheets on the bed. "I'll be fine. If you don't mind hitting the breaker, I can take care of the rest in here."

He continued staring until finally he stepped back and nodded, his hands on his hips. "Good night, Ashley."

She hugged the sheets to her. "Good night, Christopher."

He took a step toward the door when gunfire exploded outside.

"Get down!" Christopher threw her to the floor, covering her body with his.

Her heart pounded louder than a drum in her ears as

prickly fear took hold of her. What was going on? Had those men found her?

Her gaze skittered across the room. They had to hide—but where? There was only this room, a closet and a small bathroom. There was no other escape except the door they'd entered through, and stepping outside now would make them open targets.

The gunfire continued. Glass broke. A car alarm wailed. It sounded like a war outside.

She turned enough to see Christopher. She flinched when she saw the expression on his face. She'd seen a lot of expressions on him before, but never one like this. His face was tight, his eyes livid, his lips pulled into a rigid line. He looked like a cat ready to pounce.

The war. Karina had warned Ashley in their brief conversation earlier that the war had changed him. Was this what she meant?

Fear unlike anything she'd ever felt before today threatened to suffocate her. It was only a matter of time before the gunmen found them up here. It was only a matter of time before they killed her and Christopher.

Ashley scooted from beneath him and crouched by the wall. "Do you still have your gun?" she whispered.

Christopher pulled himself up and squatted beside her, alert and ready to spring into action. He shook his head. "I left it on the table inside. Wasn't planning on needing it."

"They're going to kill us." Her voice cracked as the gunfire continued. Was it her imagination or was the sound getting closer and closer?

He gripped her arm, his voice stern. "Don't say that. We'll get out of this somehow."

Was he in the same place she was? "We're sitting ducks. It's just a matter of time before they find us."

"Don't talk like that. I've gotten out of worse before."

He nodded toward the bathroom. "Stay low and go into the bathroom. We'll buy ourselves as much time as possible."

Her hands trembled against the floor as she dragged herself toward the small space. He'd gotten out of worse than this? She couldn't imagine. Didn't want to imagine.

Nausea roiled in her gut. *Lord, help us. Help David and Josh.*

Just who were these men? Why did they want her dead? How had they found her? The questions repeated themselves over and over.

Her hands connected with the cool tile of the bathroom floor. Gunshots continued to explode outside. They were trying to make sure Ashley was dead, weren't they? And out here in the country, there was no one else around to hear the commotion and come help.

Fear threatened to seize each of her muscles. Christopher jetted into the bathroom behind her and quietly shut the door. Ashley climbed into the bathtub—located against an interior wall—and Christopher sat beside her. She pulled her knees to her chest and tried to even out her breathing.

The cold air seemed to crackle with fear, with certainty of death.

Then everything went silent outside.

Ashley wasn't sure which was worse—the gunfire or the silence.

What were the gunmen doing? Had they gone inside the house to look for them, to make sure a bullet had pierced their flesh?

When they discovered Ashley wasn't there, would they come out to the garage to finish the job? She pressed herself harder into the cool tile.

Christopher leaned close enough that Ashley could feel his breath on her cheek. "Stay here. Understand?"

"Where are you going?" She grabbed his arm, desperate to keep her only known ally close—even if he had broken her heart at one time.

He locked gazes with her, that same confidence that had always made her feel safe shining in his eyes. "I'm going to find something to fight with."

"But they have guns!" She squeezed harder, her own fear creeping in.

"If I go down, I'm going to go down fighting, Ashley." His voice was steady, holding not even a hint of disbelief. "I want you to stay in here. Lock the door when I leave. Understand?"

She couldn't answer. She only stared at him silently. Despair threatened to bite deep.

"Understand?"

Finally, she nodded as reality set in.

He tried to stand but Ashley pulled him back down. "I came here for your help, not to get you killed." Her voice cracked with fear and regret. How had her life turned into this?

His eyes softened for a moment. "I know. Trust me. Okay?"

She didn't know if she could ever trust him again. But in this moment, she had no choice. She nodded. Her heart pounded in her ears as he pulled the door open. She held her breath, waiting for more gunfire to break out—only this time closer.

There was nothing.

He pointed to the lock before closing the door. Tears rolled down her face as she turned the button and heard the mechanism click in place.

*Lord, be with him. Please. He may have broken my heart, but I never wanted this.*

Something creaked outside.

The steps. Someone was coming up the steps.

Fear squeezed tighter as she braced herself for whatever was about to come.

# THREE

All Christopher had been able to find in the closet was an old metal pipe that was probably leftover from some plumbing work. It wasn't a gun or a grenade, but it would work. He didn't have any other options.

He stood on the other side of the door frame, pressed into the wall and ready to swing into action. Adrenaline surged through him, intensifying his heart rate and causing sweat to dot his forehead. If he could catch the shooter off guard, maybe he had a chance.

The problem was that he'd estimated there to be at least three shooters. All of that gunfire had come from more than one weapon. These men carried semiautomatics, and they'd brought no shortage of ammunition. One man he might be able to take. But an unarmed man taking on three men with semiautomatic weapons?

Another round of gunshots cracked the air outside of his home. Flashbacks of the Middle East pounded his memories. Mortar shells, improvised explosive devices, enemy combatants. Men bleeding, women crying, children searching for their parents.

He ran a hand over his eyes. No, he was in Virginia now. Not a dusty village in Afghanistan. So why could he practically smell the burning of C-4? Why did his skin feel gritty with sand and dust?

He shook his head. *Snap out of it, Jordan.*

But the memories continued to batter him. He squeezed his eyes shut, wishing he could turn off his thoughts as easily as turning off a TV.

Another creak on the stairs pulled him back to reality, back to the here and now. Someone was definitely coming up. Christopher gripped the pipe tighter, bracing himself for the coming struggle.

Another creak. Then another. They were getting closer. They had to be only a few steps away.

Christopher would swing as soon as they opened the door. Best-case scenario, he'd knock the man out and grab his weapon. Worst-case scenario...well, he wouldn't go there.

All he knew was that he and Ashley might be the only hope for saving a little boy. That was worth fighting for.

A wooden step outside moaned under the weight of an intruder. Whoever the man was, he was right outside the door now. Christopher could practically hear him breathing, could almost feel his presence only inches away, separated by the door.

He tightened his grip on the cylinder in his hands. His muscles were wound tight enough to spring. Sweat trickled down from his temple. It was do or die.

Just then, a bullet pierced the air. His gaze darted across the dark room. Where had that gunshot come from? It was too far away to have come from the man outside the door. Even more concerning—had it pierced the garage? Was Ashley okay?

He stared at the door, waiting to see the handle jiggle. He anticipated more shots exploding. Something hit the landing outside the door with a loud thud. A moan followed, then a grunt.

He willed himself to remain still. Everything in him wanted to open the door and see what was happening. He had to remain silent, though. Patience could mean life or death; winning a battle or losing it. He'd learned that through experience.

Afghanistan flashed into his mind again. At once, he was transported back in time and pressed against the wall of an abandoned house. Rags—or were they clothes?—were strewn across the dirty floor. The air smelled like death.

Where was Liam? Why wasn't he answering his radio? The insurgents were—

Another thud sounded outside. Christopher snapped back to reality, shaking his head to dislodge his memories of war. The thud was followed by what sounded like something large being dragged away. What in the world was happening out there? The sounds repeated for a few minutes until finally there was silence again.

He waited. And waited.

Were these men planning something else? Or had their original plans been thwarted? By what, though?

Staying low, he crept back to the bathroom. He tapped on the door once. "Ashley. It's me."

The door opened so quickly that Christopher was certain her hand had been on the knob the whole time. She practically fell into the room, fell into him. Her limbs shook with fear.

"You're alive," she whispered. She started to reach for him but stopped.

He grabbed her elbow anyway, but only to help her stay upright. "I'm fine. You okay?"

Worry stained her gaze. "What's going on? I thought…

I thought you'd been shot. I heard…" She didn't finish her thought.

His heart tugged with compassion, but he shoved those emotions aside. Right now there was only room for one thing—logic. Emotions would only lead him astray. "I don't know what happened out there. It's been quiet now for ten minutes. I don't want to take the chance that they're still out there trying to wait us out. We should lay low for a little while longer."

She nodded quickly. Christopher wanted to sit beside her, to offer her some comfort and put her mind at rest. He wished that he could distract her with chitchat—do something to keep her mind off the matters at hand. But he couldn't. Instead, he stood by the bathroom door, still gripping that pipe. The last thing he wanted was for someone to catch him off guard.

Ashley showing up today had already filled his quota on that for a lifetime.

Ashley pulled her knees to her chest, hating feeling so helpless, hating that she'd gotten Christopher into this mess. Her anxiety had her feeling nauseous and jittery. So she just kept praying the same prayers over and over again. *Lord, help us. Help David and Josh.*

Then there had been her crazy worry over Christopher. She'd heard that gunshot—it had sounded so close—and she was sure he'd been hit. All she could think about were the many unfinished conversations they needed to have. *She* needed to have.

Which caused another swell of anxiety to rise in her.

The strangest comfort filled her when she saw the pure determination on Christopher's face as he stood in the doorway. He'd always been tough and protective. They were two of the things she'd loved about him at one time.

She couldn't imagine feeling safer around anyone. But feeling physically safe was entirely different from feeling emotionally safe.

Christopher had made it clear when he left that she wasn't important to him. She obviously hadn't captured his heart enough for him to try and make their relationship work. No, true love hadn't conquered all. Or they hadn't had true love. She wasn't sure which was worse.

She wondered if he'd found his perfect woman yet, the one he would do anything to be with. That person was not her. Despite that, she knew that Christopher would give his life for her, whether she was his fiancée or just someone from his past.

She understood what it was like to feel protective of someone. Without a second thought, she would take a bullet for her nephew. Whenever they were together, it seemed like she was trying to protect him from something—viruses, bullies, drivers who weren't paying attention. She tried to protect him from other things, too, things like the heartbreak of losing his mom and loneliness from a father who worked too much.

What she wouldn't give to be able to protect him now. Her heart squeezed with pain.

Minutes ticked by. Just what was going on outside? Had the shooters given up? That just didn't seem likely. But why else would they leave? Or had they?

She hugged her knees tighter.

*Lord, help us. Help David and Josh.*

"I'm going to go down and check things out." Christopher's voice pulled her from her heavy thoughts.

New alarm spread through her. She straightened, forcing herself not to grab him. "But what if they're still there?"

His jaw flexed. "I haven't heard a sound in a half hour."

"But—"

"I'll be careful, Ashley. I've been in hostile situations before. I can handle myself."

She stared at him a moment, knowing that his mind was equally as strong and tough as his well-defined muscles and quick reflexes. She had to trust him. What other choice did she have? Finally, she nodded.

She wanted to blurt out everything on her mind before he walked to his possible death.

*Just in case you never come back, I thought you should know that I found out a month after we broke up that I was pregnant with your child. My brother adopted the baby, and his name is David. I've been wanting to tell you for years...*

She sucked on her bottom lip.

*It's your son who was snatched today.*

How exactly did someone tell her ex-fiancé that?

How did she tell him that back when they'd been young and foolish, that one night of passion had turned into a baby? The sweetest little baby that Ashley had ever laid eyes on. Giving him up for adoption had been the most gut-wrenching thing she'd ever done. But she couldn't provide for a baby. Not only had she been in college and without a job or the ability to get a job that paid more than minimum wage, but then there was the car accident that happened when David was only two months old. Ashley had spent six months in the hospital, and she'd had months of physical therapy after that. Her brother and his wife had been so desperate for a child and she'd been unable to take care of little David. They'd adopted him before his first birthday.

That's why she knew Christopher was the only person who could help her right now. This was his son.

Everything that she'd tried so carefully to control was slipping away. She couldn't protect David. She couldn't keep Christopher at a distance. She would have to face her fears and eventually tell Christopher the truth. The walls she'd so carefully constructed were coming down fast.

She sucked in a long, deep breath. Silence surrounded her again. Was Christopher okay? She'd heard nothing since he left.

At least nothing meant no gunfire, either. Right?

How long did she wait before checking on him? She glanced at her watch. Ten more minutes. That was as long as she could possibly stand it. What if he was bleeding and hurt? What if he needed her help? She'd sent him into a battle that wasn't his to fight.

She let her head fall back against the cold tile wall. All was quiet. Suspiciously quiet. The silence was driving her mad.

She stood and began pacing the small space. Maybe she could go to the window and peer out. She could be quick and quiet.

It beat sitting here and doing nothing.

Before she could second-guess herself, she twisted the doorknob. Slowly, she pushed the door open. Her gaze roamed the space there. Everything looked the same. No figures lurked in the shadows…she didn't think, at least.

She took her first step out, every cell of her body alert and ready to pounce into action. Slowly, she tiptoed across the floor to the window, not relaxing for even a second. Would someone jump out at her? Were they lying in wait?

She ducked low under the window and carefully raised her head to peer out. She flinched when she saw all of the windows in Christopher's house had been shattered. Christmas wreathes that had once graced the glass panes now lay like corpses on the deck and in the flower beds.

She watched for a sign of movement, but saw nothing. Where was Christopher? What was taking him so long?

She crawled across the floor to the closet. Was there anything left in here she could use as a weapon? She spotted a vacuum, some old coats and a wooden bar full of clothes hangers that stretched across the top. It would have to do. She stood and wedged the bar from its holders. It wasn't much, but at least it was something.

Doubt filled her as she crept toward the door. She shouldn't do this. But she had to. If they were going to shoot her, they would shoot her. But if they were gone and Christopher needed help, then she had to get downstairs.

Stark fear gripped her as she opened the door. She listened. Nothing except the wind blowing some stray leaves across the ground. Her heart leaped into her throat when she saw blood across the wooden landing at her feet.

Blood? Whose blood? What had happened? She followed the trail all the way to the bottom. Someone had been shot up here and then dragged back down. Terror rose in her.

She couldn't turn back now. If she let fear dictate what she did, she might be in the bathroom for days, afraid to leave. But each step down the stairs felt like a step closer to her death.

*Be strong, Ashley. You can do this.* She'd never been a quitter. Not even when she gave David up for adoption. No, she'd simply been giving him the opportunity for a better life—a life that she could still be a part of.

But if she hadn't given him up for adoption, would he be in this situation now? Regret squeezed her heart again. She couldn't think like that. Not now.

She continued her descent. Everything remained silent. She gripped the wooden rod like a baseball bat, wishing it would protect her from bullets.

At the bottom of the stairs, she saw that the blood trail ended at the edge of the deck. Whoever had been shot had been dragged onto the grass. Into the woods? She couldn't be sure.

She swung her head back up, soaking in her surroundings. She had to pay attention. Her life depended on it.

The back door of Christopher's house was wide open. She paused at the corner of the garage and slowly peered around. Nothing. No one. As quickly as possible, she darted across the deck. She stopped at the doorway.

With baited breath, she raked her gaze across the inside. Lots of broken glass. A splintered coffee table. The Christmas tree lay wounded on its side.

But no one was in sight. Not even Christopher.

Certainly he hadn't abandoned her. Not again.

She shook her head. No, he wouldn't do that. Not in this situation.

Still, doubt trickled down her spine. Trust was such a fragile, fickle thing at times.

She stepped inside. Glass crunched at her feet. She froze, waiting for the telltale sound that someone had heard her.

Nothing.

Slowly, carefully, she crept forward. She kept her back to the wall. Her breathing sounded so heavy in her own ears that she wondered if she'd even hear someone sneak up on her.

When she heard a noise upstairs, she knew she would.

Someone was in the house. Had that person killed Christopher, dragged his body into the woods and gone back upstairs to check for her?

Just then, the stairs creaked. Someone was coming down. Coming toward her.

She glanced around, desperate for a place to hide. Instead, she pressed herself into the wall.

When the intruder got to the bottom of the steps, she would swing the stick and hit him.

And she'd pray that her hit would knock him out.

But before she had a chance to swing, a gun cocked behind her, and the fear that was becoming all too familiar froze her blood—again.

# FOUR

Christopher approached the intruder from behind, veering off the main staircase at the last minute and taking a second set of stairs on the other end of the house. There was still one person in the house. Just one, best he could tell.

It was dark, void of any light. The air was hazy, evidence of a smoke bomb. And the smell of ammunition hung heavy in the atmosphere.

The sounds, the smells…they all reminded him of another time, another place.

A time and place he was trying to forget.

He rounded the corner and spotted someone crouching beneath the first staircase. Crouching, ready to attack?

He cocked his gun, drawing on all of his training. It was time to get some answers.

"Don't move," he commanded. "Or I'll shoot."

The figure twirled around, a stick in hand. Wide, familiar eyes met his. Fear stretched across their depths.

His muscles relaxed a moment, but the relief was quickly replaced with agitation. "Ashley? Are you crazy? I told you stay in the garage!"

"Christopher?" Ashley blinked, her stick still hoisted over her shoulder as if she might swing.

He lowered his gun and glared at the woman in front of him. Even in the dark, Christopher could tell that her face was void of any color or life. "Yes, it's me. It's a good thing I didn't shoot you. I heard the glass crunching downstairs and thought the men were back to finish the job."

"I saw the blood on the stairs. I thought you were… dead. I…"

He raised an eyebrow. "You were coming to defeat the bad guys with a dowel rod?"

She shrugged. "I had to do something. I couldn't stay up there forever."

He stepped closer so she would be sure to see the irritation in his gaze. "I told you I'd be back."

She didn't look away. She was still as stubborn as ever. "You've been gone for hours."

"Twenty minutes." He sliced his hand through the air. "Twenty minutes is all."

She frowned and lowered her stick before jutting out her chin again. "It felt like hours."

He scowled again and ran a hand over his face as he dragged in a ragged breath. Images of war continued to beat at him. They tried to transport him back in time. He wouldn't let them. Still, Ashley coming up on him like that could have been ugly. Really ugly. That was the second time he'd pulled a gun on her in less than four hours. "Are you okay?"

She nodded, strain pulling at each of her features. "I'm fine. Are the men gone?"

"Best I can tell. They messed this place up, didn't they?" His gaze roamed around them. It looked like a massacre, only thankfully, the only casualties were his furniture, belongings and the house itself.

"I'm sorry," she blurted. "I should have never come."

"Don't be ridiculous. This is just stuff. It can be fixed. Besides, you weren't the one with the gun."

Big, luminous eyes looked up to meet his. "Who was? Who were those men?"

He looked away before he got lost in the depths of those baby blues and shook his head. "I have no idea. But they mean serious business."

"Why'd they leave?"

"That's what I want to know, also. They didn't do all of this damage just to send a message. They used a smoke bomb and everything. They came here to kill us. I want to know why they left before finishing the job."

"And where did the blood come from by the garage?"

"Another great question." He put his hand on her back. "I know one thing. We're getting out of here before they decide to come back. I called Eyes and they're sending some men out. They should be here any minute, but we're not waiting around."

"Where are we going?"

"I have an idea." He led her toward the front door.

She reached back. "My phone. It was in the living room."

"Forget about it. That's probably how they traced you here. All those new-fangled phones have built-in GPSs. You're better off without it." He grabbed his jacket—surprisingly still intact—from the back of a chair.

"But what if Josh or David try to call?"

"If you're dead, it will do no good."

They stepped out of the front door—which had been ripped from its hinges—and onto the front porch. His truck had bullet holes in the window also, but the tires looked fine. "I'm glad you're wearing a coat. It might be a cold ride."

He opened the door and, using the thick sleeve of his

jacket, he brushed broken glass shards from the seat. Then he ushered Ashley inside, instructing her to be careful. They didn't have much time. Every minute counted.

He cranked the engine—and the heat—and turned around in the driveway. The cold wind hit his face as he took off down the road. Ashley sat beside him, seat belt strapped across her chest, and her arms wrapped over her. He wished he had a blanket to offer her. Instead, he pulled off his coat and draped it over her.

"You're going to freeze," she muttered.

"You're always cold, even without thirty-degree wind hitting you in the face. I'll be fine."

He remembered that about her. He remembered a lot about her. Now wasn't the time to think about those things. Now he had to think about staying alive.

This was not what he needed right now. No, right now he needed time to enjoy a quieter pace. He needed time to let his soul heal.

But instead, God had brought Ashley Wilson back into his life.

As if that wasn't more of an emotional storm than he could handle, throw in the fact that someone was trying to kill her and, in effect, him also.

This was not the relaxing, healing time he'd anticipated when he'd come home and taken this new job.

When he'd last spoken to Ashley, she'd been finishing up her degree at a local college. She'd been working two jobs, trying to make ends meet. He'd always said that she was one of the hardest workers he'd ever met. She'd been focused, at the top of her class in academics and determined to do things on her own. Her dad had retired on disability after an injury at work, and money had been tight with her family. She'd even had the opportunity to play volleyball on a partial scholarship for a college down in North Carolina, but she'd turned it down to be close to her mom, dad and brother.

Guilt plagued him about that decision. He knew part of the reason she'd said no to that scholarship was because of him. They'd been planning their future together. She'd wanted to stick close by both for her family and because she felt it was important to give their relationship the time and effort it required.

Was she angry still? He couldn't blame her if she was. He'd broken her heart.

"I can't believe this is happening," Ashley muttered.

"It feels surreal to me, too, if it makes you feel better."

She shook her head. "I just want to wake up and discover this is all a bad dream."

He wondered if by *all* she included him? Probably.

His eyes watered from the wind. Thankfully, he didn't see anyone behind him. A glance at his watch told him it was past midnight now. There wasn't usually much traffic out on these back roads, especially not at this time of night.

From the corner of his eye, he saw Ashley shivering in the seat beside him. If he'd had another vehicle, he would have driven it. But desperate times called for desperate measures. Wasn't that how the saying went?

He took back roads, all the way from Isle of Wight where he lived, through the neighboring Suffolk into Chesapeake and finally to Virginia Beach. Nearly an hour after he left, he pulled up to a guardhouse, showed his ID, had his truck searched as standard procedure and pulled through the gates.

"Where are we?" Ashley asked.

"We're at Iron, Incorporated's headquarters. You'll be safe here for the night. I promise."

Ashley stared at the huge, lodgelike building in front of her. So this was the prestigious paramilitary contracting firm she'd heard hints about. They were secretive in what they did, but people around town always whispered about them with pride. Rumors had it that they'd guarded ambassadors in the Middle East and developed cutting-edge technology that was soon to be released to help keep soldiers safer. They were said to be the best of the best.

She didn't feel like soaking in the awe of the Eyes' campus, though. She couldn't even feel her skin anymore, not after the brutal wind had frozen it on the way here. All she wanted was to get off this roller-coaster ride for a moment and clear her head.

When they pulled to a stop, she didn't wait for Christopher to get her door. Instead, she opened it, watching as some leftover glass rained to the ground below. She slid out, landing with a bounce on the asphalt.

They started walking toward the door when Christopher called her name and stopped her. He reached for her hair. Just the feeling of his fingers tangled in her tresses caused a shiver to race down her spine. It was like her body was betraying her. It should know better than to get warm fuzzies about Christopher, especially after all that had happened.

He held up a shiny speck. "Just some glass."

She nodded, stuffed her hands in her pockets and kept walking. Christopher hurried ahead to the door and pulled it open for her. She gladly stepped inside the quiet and warm space. Her gaze swept the area—the ceiling stretched more than two stories high. Fireplaces flanked either side of the large lobby, which was also filled with leather couches and plush rugs. A majestic Christmas tree stretched high in the corner, filled with ornaments that looked like they'd been made by schoolchildren. She didn't have time to dwell on that now. She walked over to the fireplace and knelt in front of it, letting the heat melt her frozen limbs.

"I'm going to get coffee," Christopher called. "You still like yours black?"

She nodded, holding her hands up to the flames. He remembered. What did she expect? That he'd totally forgotten about their time together? That he'd erased it from his memory?

He returned a moment later with a steaming mug. She remained in front of the fire and took a sip. The liquid burned her mouth, but she didn't care. Warmth was more important now. Maybe it would cause her shivers to finally stop.

"I've got to make a phone call, Ashley. Are you going to be okay here for a moment?"

She nodded again, wishing he wasn't acting so concerned. It was easier not to like him if he acted mean and nasty. But when had he ever been mean and nasty?—unless you counted when he broke up with her. But even then, he'd been compassionate. His eyes had even welled with tears at one point.

The day flashed back into her memory. She could tell that something was wrong when he'd called her by phone. His voice had sounded too serious, too strained.

*He's going to tell me he's going to the Middle East again,* she'd thought.

She'd braced herself for the conversation, fluctuating between wanting to be supportive and wanting to beg him to stay.

*Be a good fiancée. Accept that this is his job. Let him go, even if it means postponing the wedding.*

He'd asked if they could meet down at the Virginia Beach boardwalk—one of their favorite places. She'd bundled up—it was cold outside—and waited for him on their favorite bench. Die-hard joggers had paced past, seagulls had complained overhead, salty air had filled her nostrils.

As soon as she'd seen Christopher walking toward her, she could tell something was wrong.

Her spine had stiffened. *This is about more than Afghanistan, isn't it?* But what? In their two years together, they'd never even had a major fight. That's how easy and natural their relationship had been.

Those expressive green eyes had held torn emotions as he sat beside her. His shoulders even looked burdened. "I can't be with you, Ashley," he'd told her.

"What do you mean?"

"I've realized that I can't be a good SEAL and a good husband."

"What are you talking about?" She'd blinked back her confusion, certain that she hadn't heard him correctly. What he said didn't make sense.

He'd grabbed her hand. "You're the only person I want to be with, Ashley. But that's not fair to my country. I promised them I would protect our freedoms. I'm not doing that when I'm thinking about you. Being a SEAL…it's almost like being married. And I've already made that commitment."

"You're breaking up with me?" Her voice had cracked in disbelief. How had things gone from perfect to this?

Water had filled his eyes. "I'm sorry, Ashley. I've been pretending I could do both, but it's become clear that I can't."

She snapped back to the present and the blazing fire in front of her. Funny, she hadn't thought about Christopher's tear-filled eyes in a long time. Oh, she'd thought about the breakup, but somehow she'd blocked out memories of how anguished he'd looked during their conversation. Christopher was the last person she wanted to be thinking about right now.

She dragged her mind from one bad thought to another—David. Where was he right now? Was he warm? Comfortable? Had they fed him?

She took another sip of coffee, her hands still trembling as her heart ached.

*Please, Lord, don't let him be scared.*

As anxiety squeezed her, she nearly dropped her coffee when a hand reached out and grabbed it. She looked up and saw Christopher there. Just in the nick of time. Again. Like always.

Except when he'd left her.

She had to stop thinking about that and start concentrating solely on the matters at hand. Her heart was just in such a fragile state right now that it kept going other places. Christopher helped her into a plush chair. She set her coffee on the table, unsure if her hands could hold it any longer.

"Two of the guys from Eyes are coming down. Jack and Denton. They're still here, working on a big project for the Department of Defense. They're the best. They'll be able to help."

"Thank you," she mumbled. After a few minutes of silence stretched between them, she asked, "How'd you end up here, Christopher? I never thought you'd leave the military. I thought you'd be a career guy."

A new somberness seemed to come over him. "So did I. But life changes sometimes. It was time."

"How long have you been back?"

"Three months." He changed the subject. "How about you? You still a web designer?"

She nodded. "Started my own business about five years ago."

"You're a business owner now?"

"I was working for a corporation, but I was miserable. Great benefits, great pay, but no fulfillment, you know what I mean? So I took a leap of faith and started my own company. I design websites for some major companies, all while working in the luxury of my own home. I've been really blessed."

A smile spread over his face. "I know that's what you always wanted to do. I'm glad you were able to."

"Yeah, at least some things worked out according to plan." She clamped her mouth shut. Now why had she gone and said that? It wasn't very mature of her. She glanced at her hands. "I'm sorry."

"I deserved it."

"No, you didn't. I don't know what's gotten into me."

"All of this is a lot to handle. I think you're doing just fine."

Her gaze connected with his. "It's only by God's grace we're alive, isn't it?"

"I couldn't agree more."

She stared at him. He meant those words, didn't he? When they'd known each other before, neither had been Christians. She must have stared at him long enough that he felt obligated to give an explanation.

"When you've seen some of the things that I saw over in the Middle East, you start believing there's a God pretty quickly."

"I'd imagine." *When you have to give your child up for adoption, you start believing pretty quickly, too.* She kept that part to herself.

Just then, two men tromped down the stairs. She drew in a deep breath, ready to formulate a plan to get her brother and son back.

\* \* \*

Jack Sergeant, the CEO of Eyes, and Mark Denton, his second in command, came to a stop in front of them. Both looked like they'd been working long hours. They'd abandoned their ties and coats. The top button of Denton's white shirt was open and the shadow of a beard had already formed on his cheeks.

Mark—who went by Denton—had helped to train Christopher as a SEAL before going to work for the CIA. He'd been Christopher's contact in getting a job here and, for that, Christopher was grateful.

Christopher trusted Jack and Denton more than if they'd been brothers. Both had been SEALs and had earned reputations as being trustworthy and loyal, as well as innovative and at the top of their game in the paramilitary contracting world. He'd jumped at the chance to come work for them.

They introduced themselves to Ashley. Jack put his hands on his hips, his brow furrowed with concern. "What's going on?"

Ashley glanced at Christopher before sucking in a deep breath and telling her story. Even though she had to be exhausted and scared, she maintained a calm demeanor that he could appreciate. Except for her voice cracking a few times, she stuck to the facts.

Denton stepped forward. "Is there anything you can remember about the car?"

She nodded. "The license plate number."

Christopher raised his eyebrows. "You can?"

She nodded again. "I thought the police were the only ones who could do something with that information, though. I figured it would do us no good."

Jack shook his head. "We'll look into it. You have no idea who these men are?"

Ashley shook her head. "No, I have no idea. We're just simple, everyday people. Things like this don't happen to us."

Jack grunted. Christopher knew that he understood what it was like when simple, everyday people got mixed up in things bigger than they seemed equipped to handle. That was how Jack had met the woman who was now his wife, for that matter. At least that reminded Christopher of how good things could come from bad situations, similar to the flower garden he'd stumbled upon in the middle of a military base. Some soldiers had decided to make the place feel like home and planted roses and hollyhocks and other varieties he couldn't identify. How they'd made those flowers grow in that soil, he'd never know. But they had, and they'd proven to him that from the dust something beautiful could grow.

"You're both welcome to stay here for as long as you need to," Jack started. "Christopher, the men are at your place now, checking things out and boarding up your windows. You did the right thing by leaving immediately. In the meantime, we'll look into that license plate number and see what we can find out." He glanced at Ashley. "Why don't you give us your address and a house key? We'll search your place also, just to make sure there's nothing we're missing."

"I appreciate it." Her gaze met each person's in the circle while her hand clutched the necklace at her throat. "I appreciate all of your help. I have no idea what I'm doing."

Jack patted her arm. "We're glad you're here. Let us know if you need anything else." He offered a curt wave before he headed back up the stairs.

Denton lingered, his gaze meeting Christopher's. "Christopher, can I speak with you for a moment?"

Christopher nodded and followed him to a corner. He

glanced back at Ashley and saw that she'd already gravitated back toward the fire again. By the set of her shoulders, she looked like she was carrying a weight far heavier than she should bear.

He turned back to Denton. "What is it?"

Denton lowered his voice. "Are you sure you can handle this?" His eyes showed that he was dead serious.

"Of course." Christopher wasn't sure what his superior was getting at.

Denton crossed his arms and shifted, his voice still low and conspirative. "You took this job to recover from war. You're being thrown right back into a battle, though."

Christopher straightened. "I can handle it."

"I know you think you're tough. You are tough. But even the toughest soldiers have to step away from the battle sometimes."

"Sometimes a soldier has no choice but to go back into the fight. They have to reach down inside and find strength, even when they don't think they have it. That's what one of the men who once trained me said, at least." He kept his chin raised and stood at full attention, though he knew Denton would tell him to be at ease.

Denton stared at him a moment before nodding. A smile stretched across his face and he gripped his arm. Denton had been that man who said those words. "I'm here for you if you need me."

"You always have been. I appreciate that, sir."

Denton leaned closer. "Listen, I don't know what your past relationship is with Ashley, but I get the feeling you two were more than friends."

"Yes, we were. We were engaged, to be exact."

His eyes widened a moment. "This was the girl you were crazy about while you were in training, huh? I remember the way you talked about her like she was the best thing to ever happen to you."

"She was the best thing to ever happen to me." His heart squeezed as he said the words. They were true. Walking away from Ashley had felt like walking away from his heart.

"Don't let your past get in the way of doing what you have to do."

"Yes, sir." He glanced back over at Ashley. Those words would be the hardest to follow through on. Remembering their time together was so bittersweet.

Somehow, he had to ignore the fact that she hated him and realize that God had brought her back into his life for some reason…maybe even just forgiveness and closure? He didn't know.

But he did know that, in Christ, all things worked together for His good.

Somehow, someway, something good was going to come out of all of this.

The question was…what?

# FIVE

Christopher stared at the alarm clock on the nightstand beside his bed. The red numbers stared back at him. Six-twenty, and he was wide awake.

He'd been wide-awake for a long time.

For most of the night, for that matter.

He tossed toward the other side of his bed, trying to grab a few more minutes of rest. Back at home, there was a bottle of sleeping pills lying on his nightstand. He'd refused to take them, despite his doctor's encouragement. He liked to think he was strong enough to weather the storms of life without the help of any medication.

Even if he'd had the pills with him now, he wouldn't have taken any last night. He wanted to be on guard.

Between his return home, the unexpected reappearance of Ashley in his life, and the danger surrounding her, sleep had just been a dream.

He should be used to it. He hadn't had a good night's rest in months. Too many images from Afghanistan haunted him.

He'd gone to counseling all of four times, and it hadn't done him any good. All the counselor had wanted to do was talk about things. He was tired of talking about things. He just wanted to move on.

Being back in the States was an entirely different kind of battleground.

*Hang on to the good memories,* he reminded himself, punching his pillow with his fist.

He was thankful that Jack had given him a job at Eyes as a Training Specialist. He hoped his soul would have time to heal away from the battleground. But now he'd been thrust into the face of danger again, it seemed. But how could he turn Ashley away? He couldn't.

Ashley's face drifted into his mind. They'd had some good times together—some really good times, actually. Their relationship had been so simple, filled with long walks, road trips and movie marathons.

Then things had ended. No, make that, then *he'd* ended things.

He never thought he'd see her again. Or if he did see her again, he expected her to be married with kids in tow. She was the kind of woman who'd make a great mother and wife. He knew that's all she'd dreamed of for so long. She had everything a guy could want. So why was she still single? And why had she come to him of all people? Was there something she wasn't telling him? He couldn't even begin to fathom what that thing might be.

Finally, after tossing and turning for thirty more minutes, he dragged himself out of bed and hopped in the shower. Someone had left some clothes outside his door. He quickly put on the jeans and sweatshirt, making a mental note that he needed to run to the store and buy a few things today.

He stepped outside his room and stared at the door beside his. Ashley's room. It was only 7:00 a.m. Was Ashley awake yet? She'd always been an early riser. She liked to go jogging or biking before starting her day. He remembered many mornings when they'd met at the beach to run together on the boardwalk. Those memories seemed like an entirely different lifetime ago.

He raised his hand to knock at her door but stopped. He would let her sleep, or at the very least, have some privacy. When she was ready, she'd come downstairs. He needed some coffee and a bite to eat. Maybe that would wake him up. At the end of the hallway, he peered out the window and saw at least two inches of snow piled on top of everything, cloaking the landscape in innocence.

The weather forecaster had gotten it right for once. What did you know?

A blazing fire greeted him downstairs as he made his way toward the kitchen. The space was already filled with a group of law-enforcement trainees. He recognized several and waved hello. He'd been one of their instructors and had been teaching them about use of force. That responsibility had been passed on to someone else until this ordeal with Ashley subsided.

He began pouring himself a cup of coffee when he heard someone behind him.

"Christopher."

He turned away from the coffeepot at the sound of Ashley's voice, making sure any sign of his exhaustion disappeared from his face.

She stood in front of him, her eyes wide and crystal clear and as breathtaking as ever. Man, she was beautiful with that oval face, pert nose and glossy hair. If anything, the years had only made her more attractive. He could stare at her all day, and it would never get old.

"Morning, Ashley." He raised his mug. "Care for some coffee?"

She nodded and crossed her arms over her chest. He had the crazy desire to pull her into a hug, to stroke her hair and tell her everything would be okay. But he couldn't do that. Ashley Wilson was off-limits. She was now, and she should have been ten years ago.

He forced his thoughts to go in another direction. He focused on the here and the now. He knew he couldn't forget the past—and that he shouldn't—but right now he just couldn't deal with it. "Grab a plate. Breakfast is on the house."

She hesitated, but only for a moment, before putting some eggs and fruit on her plate. They sat down together at a table by the window. She thanked him before closing her eyes. Was she praying?

She pulled her eyes open, her gaze dull as it met his. "I wish they'd taken me and not David," she blurted.

"It doesn't sound like they want to kill him, Ashley. They could have already killed them both, but they haven't. Instead, they're just using that threat as leverage for you not to tell. No, I think they want your brother and David for another reason."

She nodded. "That makes sense, I guess. I just wish they'd left David out of it. He's so young and innocent. He always tries to be so tough, though. He's a real soldier—or trouper, I suppose." Her gaze met his. What was that emotion in her eyes? Regret, it almost seemed. But why?

Christopher looked up as Mark Denton approached the table with that cocky swagger he was known for. He pulled back a chair. "Mind if I sit down?"

Using his foot, Christopher pushed a chair out for him. "Please do."

Denton pulled the seat to the end of the table and straddled it. His gaze met Ashley's. "We got a trace on that license plate."

Her eyes brightened. "What did you discover?"

"It turns out the man who owns the car is named Gil Travis. Have you ever heard of him?"

Ashley shook her head. "Gil Travis? The name doesn't sound familiar."

Denton's lips pulled into a tight, grim line. "He's on the FBI's most-wanted list."

She blinked, as if trying to process his words. "What?"

Denton nodded. "He's affiliated with a terrorist organization called His People. Do you remember the bombing of that federal building up in Richmond several years ago?"

Christopher was well aware of who the group was. That particular story had made national news after five people had died.

Ashley nodded also. "Yeah, I remember that. It was all over the news."

"His People were behind it. They're determined to take down the America we know and love. They're some dangerous men, and Gil is their second in command—more of a tactical commander who plans their attacks against targets here in the U.S., as well as at embassies overseas."

"Why? Why does this group hate America so much?" Ashley asked.

Denton grimaced. "The organization formed in the 1970s under the leadership of Abar Numair—"

"He's the man who was killed several months ago, right? By some of the U.S. special forces?"

Denton briefly glanced at Christopher before nodding. "That's correct. This organization has cells all over the world, including some here in the U.S. Most of the people who join the organization have some kind of ties to the Middle East."

"Are they Islamic extremists?" Ashley asked.

Denton shook his head again. "No, that's the surprising part. Probably twenty percent of their membership is Muslim. The real reason these men have come together is that they have some kind of bone to pick with the U.S. Gil, for example. His dad was killed in a drone attack over in Iraq. His mother remarried and moved to the United States, making him a citizen—a citizen with a huge grudge."

"People with grudges can do terrible things," Ashley mumbled.

"Authorities are still trying to figure out who provides their funding for them. That's what makes them scary— there are some unknown members who stay secret." Denton pulled out a photo. "Do you recognize him?"

Ashley studied the photo for a minute. Christopher immediately recognized the tall man with a head full of dark hair, cold, black eyes and sunken cheeks. "He looks vaguely familiar, but no."

"That's Gil Travis," Denton said.

Ashley's gaze met Denton's. "I still don't understand. What does my brother have to do with this? It just doesn't make sense."

Denton drew in a deep breath. "We're still trying to figure that out. What did you say your brother did for a living again?"

"He programs computers. He's one of the best—" Her eyes widened as she stopped midsentence. "He's one of the best in the country," she finished softly. She turned toward Christopher, licking her lips. "He could hack into almost any system."

"Including the government's," Denton filled in.

"He wouldn't do that." She swung her head back and forth. "He's too ethical. Especially now that he's a dad...."

Christopher seemed to remember that Josh had gotten into trouble in high school for doing some hacking, but that was a long time ago. People changed, especially when they became parents. Certainly Josh wouldn't do anything to put his son in jeopardy.

"If he had a gun to his head, he might." Denton leaned

toward her. "We're going to need to find out some information from you, Ashley."

"Sure. I'll share anything." She grimaced after she said the words. What was that about, Christopher wondered?

Denton leaned toward her. "Tell me about your brother."

"He's the classic computer nerd. He's an absolute whiz at anything computer-related. TechShare recruited him to work for them four or five years ago."

"TechShare?" Denton questioned.

"They're some computer company. I hadn't heard of them, either, before Josh got a job with them. Apparently, they design some of the processors that the bigger companies buy. I don't know. He doesn't really like to talk about his work. He says it's boring."

Denton watched her closely, almost as if he were a human lie detector. "How about his family? Tell me about them."

"His wife died a few years ago from cancer. I'm his only sibling. My mom passed away nearly a decade ago, and my dad is living in a retirement community down in South Carolina now."

"Just one child?" Denton continued. He took a sip of coffee, his gaze never leaving hers.

She licked her lips again. "Just one. A son named David. He's eight."

"Anything we need to know about him?"

Her cheeks flushed. "He...he's, um...he's adopted. You don't think that has anything to do with this, do you?"

Denton shrugged. "Who knows? Anything's a possibility now. Was it an open or closed adoption?"

"Open."

"Do you know the birth mother's name?" Christopher turned toward Ashley, feeling like they could be onto something. "Maybe we could start there. We could find her and see if she has anything to do with this."

"I can…I can try to get her name for you. I doubt it would do any good. I think you're looking in the wrong direction."

Christopher stared at her another moment, wondering why she was acting so strangely. Earlier, she'd seemed so anxious to do whatever was necessary. Now hesitancy seemed to lace each movement. "We need to explore every possibility, Ashley."

"I agree." She rubbed her temples before finally pointing behind her. "Do you mind if I run to the restroom for a moment?"

Denton leaned back and crossed his arms over his chest. "Not at all."

She fled so quickly that she nearly knocked over a chair. Why had she reacted so strangely to that question? Perhaps it was just the stress of everything that was getting to her. So what if David had been adopted? He knew that Josh and his wife were having trouble getting pregnant. Many couples turned to adoption. So why was Ashley acting so flustered by the question?

He turned toward Denton. "This whole situation doesn't look good, does it?"

Denton shook his head grimly, tapping his pen against the side of the coffee mug. "No, not at all. These are some serious men we're dealing with. They're ruthless, cold and will stop at nothing to get what they want."

Hearing Denton say the words aloud made cold fear course through Christopher. Ashley was somehow caught up in the middle of this, and he didn't like that one bit. "Where's this leave Ashley?"

"As soon as they figure out where she is, they'll try to kill her. I don't recommend staying in one place for very long. These men have a lot of resources. They'll close in eventually. I just can't tell you when."

Christopher nodded. Yep, it was even worse than he'd ever imagined.

Ashley splashed some water on her face, trying to calm herself down. She let the water drop from the tip of her nose into the basin of the porcelain sink. Her hands, white-knuckled, gripped the edges of the counter like a life preserver. Fitting, since she felt like she was hanging on for every last breath.

They might have to look into David's adoption records, just to rule out the idea that his birth mom had nothing to do with this? Now that was something she hadn't expected to hear. How was she going to get around this? Or would she?

She had to pull herself together. She'd do whatever she had to do to get her son back. And that was that. If that meant that she had to face the mistakes of her past head-on, then that's what she'd do. But she wouldn't like it.

She grabbed a paper towel and blotted her face before pausing to stare at herself in the mirror. She looked like she'd aged ten years overnight. How things could change in the blink of an eye.

John 14:27 slipped into her mind. *Peace I leave with you; my peace I give to you. Not as the world gives do I give to you. Let not your hearts be troubled, neither let them be afraid.*

Yet all her heart felt was troubled and afraid.

*Please, Lord, help me to trust that everything is in Your hands. Give me the wisdom to know what to do next. Give me the courage to have conversations that might rock Christopher's world.*

For good measure, she wiped one more paper towel over

her face and glanced at her reflection once more. Hollow eyes, pale skin and dull hair. She'd imagined running into Christopher again after their breakup and looking fabulous, making him want to eat his heart out. Instead, he was probably glad he'd gotten away while he could. If only that worry was her biggest problem right now.

She pushed the door open and trudged back through the lobby and into the cafeteria. Denton was gone and it was just Christopher sipping his coffee. She slid into the chair across from him and stared at her eggs, which were now cold and unappealing. Instead, she stabbed a piece of pineapple with her fork.

She could feel Christopher's gaze on her. Surprisingly, she didn't feel shaken by his scrutiny. Some intrinsic part of her still seemed to trust the man and find strength from him.

Which made no sense whatsoever.

"You okay?"

"Just feeling a little shaken." She took a bite of the fruit. "Denton's gone?"

"He had to take a phone call."

She put her fork back on her plate, her appetite totally gone. Even the pineapple, one of her favorite foods, couldn't whet her appetite. "What's next?"

Christopher's green eyes studied her a moment. "It would really help if there was anything you could remember about David's birth parents. There might be a connection there that will help us find him now."

She nodded, her throat burning. Did he suspect that he was connected to David at all? She didn't think so. "I don't know what to say."

His gaze pierced hers. "Did you ever meet her?"

"In a vague sort of way, I suppose you could say that." Nausea roiled in her gut. Should she simply tell him the truth? Just drop the news on him here and now and get all of her secrets out in the open? The words wouldn't leave her throat.

Christopher pressed his palms into the table and leaned toward her, his eyes narrowed in confusion. "What does that mean, Ashley? Is something wrong?"

*Tell him. Just tell him.*

She opened her mouth, ready to share the truth. But instead, she blurted, "I'm just not feeling that great. I'm sorry." She ran a hand over her face before straightening. Maybe she could ease into the information. Fear threatened to strangle her, and she couldn't seem to take a hold of the emotion. "Okay. Let's see. I think she was young. Maybe 19 or 20. She was single. Any other information you'd have to get from the court files. I can't help you. But I can say that I think we're looking in the wrong direction. Nothing about his birth mother screamed terrorist."

"How about his dad? Did you ever meet his dad?"

Her throat burned again. "He seemed perfectly...normal. You know, I really think we should look in other directions." Fear won. Ashley couldn't tell him. Not now. All of these years, she'd made Christopher out to be the bad guy when, in truth, what she'd done had probably been worse.

It was going to be heartbreaking for her to come to terms with that truth.

Christopher stared at her for a moment before nodding. "I see."

Their gazes met and tension stretched between them.

"Bad news, guys." They both turned toward Denton as he strode into the room. He stopped in front of them, his expression grim. He turned toward Ashley. "I sent someone to check on your car this morning. You said you left it behind that shopping center off Military Highway?"

She nodded.

He slapped a picture onto the table. "It's demolished."

She blinked, her face growing even paler, as she stared at the unrecognizable piece of charred metal in the picture. "Demolished?"

"Someone set it on fire." Denton shifted. "We also sent someone to your apartment. Your desk has been cleared. I can only assume there was a computer there at one time."

She nodded. "That's right. I do all of my web design on that computer."

"I'm sorry to tell you this, but it's gone now."

She couldn't pull her eyes from the image of her charred car in front of her. "Why would they do that to my car? Why would they take my computer?"

Christopher put his hand on her arm, pulling her back to reality. "Because they want to send a message, Ashley. They want to let you know they're not done with you yet."

# SIX

Ashley huddled beneath her coat in an SUV that Denton had let them use. They needed to go and buy some items to use until this whole nightmare ended. Clothes, toiletries, shoes—they only had what they'd fled with. It wasn't safe to go to either of their places to retrieve anything.

Wind swept in from the open door in the driver's seat as Christopher climbed in beside her. He slammed the door and cranked the engine. Christmas music blared on the radio, and cool air gusted at full power through the vents.

He blew on his fingers, his breath forming frosty puffs that matched the sky around them. "It will take a few minutes for this to heat up." That apologetic look appeared in Christopher's eyes again.

Ashley nodded, pulling her coat tighter and staring out the window at the white surrounding them. The frigid weather seemed to match the chill that started at her core and spread through her veins every time she thought about Josh and David.

"It's going to be okay, Ashley." Christopher's voice broke through her brittle thoughts, pulling her back to the present.

She cleared her throat, pushing away the emotions that came upon hearing the genuine concern in his voice. "I have no idea what's going on or what we're going to do. Nothing feels okay."

He stared at her a moment. She could feel his eyes on her, but she didn't look up, didn't want him to see the fear in her gaze. She already knew what his eyes looked like— big and green and warm. She studied them a million times in the past, absorbing their every fleck and every emotion they conveyed.

"You're right, Ashley. Nothing does feel okay. All of this is crazy. We're just going to take it step by step."

There he went again. He had a way of making her feel like everything would be fine. At one time he'd been her rock, her best friend and the man who made her heart do cartwheels. Now he was going to be her bodyguard—and that was it. She needed boundaries unless she wanted to get her heart broken again. There had always been something unseen between them, some force that pulled them together that made them forget about the rest of the world. They'd had that elusive, ever-desired "it" factor that so many love songs had been written about. She'd thought they were soul mates.

It was obvious that the invisible pull between them could easily draw them together again if she let it. This time, she wasn't a little girl. She was a grown woman, not one given to whims or flights of fancy or delusions of romance. No, next time she fell in love, she'd do it using her brain. And her brain constantly reminded her of how wrong Christopher was for her, despite how her heart might protest.

Somehow her life had turned into something fit for a movie—a terribly frightening movie. Just two days ago her biggest worry had been whether she should go to the gym or watch her favorite Christmas movie. What she wouldn't give for life to be like that again. "I just want to find Josh and David."

"If you find them, then you find the men who want to kill you. Not a good idea. Let Jack and Denton handle it. They're good at what they do."

She shook her head, the answers becoming clear in her mind. "No, that's the thing. I need to find my brother and nephew *before* the men who snatched them find me. I just can't sit around and do nothing. It's not an option. I need to be proactive. I'll rent a car—"

"If you use a credit card, they'll be able to trace you."

"I'll borrow a car, then. Certainly one of the families at church has an extra one I could use."

"You risk pulling them into the middle of this mess. And, even if you find a car, then what?"

She mulled over his words. It was true. She couldn't risk pulling anyone else into the middle of this. But if she could find a car, somehow and someway, maybe she could form a plan. "If I can find a car, I'll drive until an answer smacks me in the face." She sighed and rubbed her temples as the futility of her plan hit her. "They make this look so easy in the movies."

"Life isn't a movie. Movies are nice and tidy bundles with everything resolved at the end. Life is messy and tangled with very few certainties. Our next breath isn't promised, no matter who we are."

"That sounds like a fact you know all too well." She'd heard through a couple of mutual acquaintances that they'd lost a member of their SEAL team during one of their raids. Christopher hadn't mentioned it yet in their brief time together, but Ashley knew his world had been turned upside down when that happened. The brotherhood of the SEAL teams was amazing, a fact she'd seen firsthand when she and Christopher were engaged. Losing someone on your team was like losing a family member.

His lips pulled into a tight line. "Unfortunately, I do."

Grim reality set in around her. How would all of this turn out? She had to believe for the best. Otherwise, hopelessness would paralyze her.

They needed to search for answers at Ground Zero, she realized.

"I know where to start," she muttered.

"Where's that?" He stared at her, tension stretching between them. She knew him well enough to know that one of his biggest stressors had always been worrying about her safety. His laidback attitude always disappeared if he thought she might be in danger—physically, emotionally, mentally—whatever the case. At least, that's the way it used to be.

She raised her chin. It wasn't his job to worry about her anymore. She could take care of herself. "My brother's house."

"I don't know if that's a good idea." His lips pulled into a tight, grim line.

"Do you have any others?" She tried to keep the edge from her voice, but emotion threatened to burst through. She couldn't sit idly by while David and Josh were in danger.

"Yeah, keep you safe. Tuck you away somewhere until this storm has passed." Somewhere in his voice she heard a touch of that protectiveness that she'd always loved. But he had no reason to be protective of her now. They were two estranged friends who'd been thrown together again after years apart. In those years, they'd changed; they'd become new people. And once this was over, they'd go back to the way things had been.

"You know I'm not a sit back and stay quiet kind of girl,

Christopher." Outside the window, the landscape morphed from back roads into suburban housing developments and shopping centers.

He smiled. "Yeah, I know."

She crossed her arms over her chest. "There is a back way to get into Josh's house."

He looked into the distance and sighed. "I'm stating for the record that I have reservations about this."

"You know I'm going to do it with or without you."

"Exactly."

She stared at him, waiting for his response. Finally, he nodded. "I'm calling some men from Eyes in to check things out first. And we're not making any moves until it gets dark outside."

Christopher watched as Ashley picked up a blue sweater and raised it in the air. Her eyes narrowed as if she was imagining herself in it before she draped it over her arm and continued looking.

That method of determining what she wanted would have to do for now. They didn't have time to try on any clothes. They had to get what they needed and keep moving.

Christopher had decided to come to a local mall to do their shopping. What better place to blend in than the throngs of people out looking for last-minute Christmas gifts. How far away was Christmas again? A week?

He hadn't been looking forward to the holiday. His mom was out of town. His dad had been out of his life for two decades. His grandfather was dead. Christopher had planned on spending the day alone, reflecting on life—the past, the future, his failures, his successes, his regrets, his victories. Then he'd pray he could leave all of those things at the feet of a God who'd been born in a stable, but had grown to be the Savior of the world and his reason for hope.

He'd convinced himself that being alone was what he wanted, though he knew it wasn't the truth. He'd made his choices. He'd traded a family for his career.

And now his career was over, and he was left with what felt like nothing.

He glanced around him once more, as he'd been doing since they arrived. He might actually enjoy a day like this, if it wasn't for the circumstances that had brought them there. Garlands and evergreens decorated the countertops and columns and displays. "We Wish You a Merry Christmas" rang out through the speakers. Excitement seemed to zing through the air. The holiday rush—wasn't that what people called it?

As Ashley stepped away, Christopher remained close. Anyone watching would think they were a couple out shopping together. No one would guess their history. It wasn't every day that God brought you the chance to make things right. The most he could hope for was Ashley's forgiveness. He'd ruined any possibility of a second chance, of Ashley being in his life again. But it didn't matter. He was too messed up from the war. He feared too much that he'd let Ashley down again, just like his own father had let Christopher down when he walked away from their family.

Despite that, there was so much he and Ashley needed to talk about, but now wasn't the time. Now they just had to concentrate on staying alive.

Christopher's mind raced back in time to trips they had made together a decade ago. Even doing simple things like grocery shopping together had been fun with Ashley. She had a way of offering commentary on the most mundane things, making routines seem entertaining.

Back then, they'd wanted to be together as much as possible.

She'd always said it wasn't the big things in life that you remembered. It was the small, everyday things that were important.

When he thought back to their time together, it was the simple things about their relationship that made him smile—things like jogging together, picking out the perfect apple, watching the sunrise and searching for seashells along the bay.

He shook his head, snapping back to the present. His gaze scanned the store. Two men walked in together and immediately separated. Christopher saw the way they glanced at each other, as if communicating in some unspoken way. Both perused shirts at opposite sides of the store. Funny, because the trendy clothes here looked nothing like what the suited men would wear.

Christopher gripped Ashley's arm. "We need to go."

She looked up, startled. "What do you mean?"

"I mean, they've found us."

She dropped the sweater as Christopher pulled her toward the back of the store. They slipped past the dressing rooms and into the office. All the employees were on the sales floor, busy helping with the Christmas rush, so there was no one to stop them.

He pushed through a back entrance that led to a hallway that ran behind the stores—usually reserved only for employees. As soon as their feet hit the tile there, he grabbed Ashley's hand and began running. "We've got to get out of here!"

Just as they rounded a corner, someone else emerged from the doorway. Shots rang out, echoing in the small space.

In a mall? These men were shooting at them in a mall? They meant serious business.

"Come on!" He pulled her into a store. Would those men be as brazen as to shoot at them in plain sight?

*Please, Lord, keep everyone safe, not just us.*

He sucked in a breath when he realized they'd stepped into a hair salon. The minimally decorated store offered no cover. As they emerged from the back, all the customers and stylists inside stared at them from their booths.

Christopher kept a tight hold of Ashley's hand, pulling her through the space until they reached the crowded mall. He skidded to a halt after stepping into the ocean of people toting shopping bags and oversize coats.

Where were those men? It was only a matter of time before they found them again. They had to hide.

Now.

To their right was a "pictures with Santa" area. He had to lead the shooters away from that display, just in case the men started shooting again. He pulled Ashley toward the food court instead. He plunged into the middle of the crowd, hoping to stay concealed.

From behind them, he heard a yell.

Then more gunfire erupted.

Screams scattered throughout the crowd. People ducked or ran or cried out or did all three.

Christopher and Ashley burst into a sprint. They were on the second floor. They had to get downstairs and out to the car. Two mall-security officers ran past, radios in hand.

But the two gunmen kept shooting.

Who were they?

And if they were desperate to kill Ashley so they wouldn't be discovered, then why were they shooting at her in a mall where they would be discovered? There had to be more to this than either of them realized.

He'd think about that later. Right now, they had to stay alive.

The escalators were just ahead. Going downstairs would be risky, but what other choice did they have?

A bullet grazed past his arm, and he pulled tighter on Ashley's hand. "Stay with me here!"

Just before he got on the escalator, he pulled a trash can down behind him and created an obstacle that would hopefully gain them a few extra seconds. He took the steps by two, slowing only enough to keep his balance. Another shot was fired.

When they reached the bottom, he grabbed the emergency off switch. The escalator came to a halt, and the two men tumbled downward at the loss of motion.

He used their stumble as an opportunity to pull Ashley into a department store.

He glanced back in time to see a mall cop grab one of the men. The man swung his gun around and aimed it right at the security officer. Then Christopher heard the blast of another bullet being fired.

*Oh, Lord, help us all.*

Ashley let out a small cry behind him. She'd seen it also.

Shoppers huddled behind displays of toasters and blenders. Others ran toward the doors.

They weren't going to be able to outrun the gunmen, Christopher realized. They were too close on their heels. Even if they made it outside, they'd be goners in the empty stretch of parking lot between the mall and the cars. The men would catch them.

"This way." He pulled Ashley toward the housewares section, looping around and hopefully throwing the men off their trail for a moment. He had to find a place to hide. Now.

Finally, he saw something that might conceal them—for a moment, at least. He eased a display mattress off its frame. "Get in. Quick."

Ashley climbed into the wood frame and ducked down. He quickly crawled in beside her and pulled the mattress back over.

He prayed that the outside of the bedding display was straight enough that no one would notice he'd moved it. He'd tried to be careful.

"What are we doing?" Fear strained Ashley's voice. He could only see her outline as faint slivers of light crept through small gaps in the wood frame.

"We can't outrun them, Ashley. We've got to lose their trail and then take off."

He scooted closer to one of those gaps and peered out. It was hard to make out anything, but he saw policemen running past. Good. The police had been called in. That might make the men run. He could hope.

"How'd they find us?" Ashley whispered.

"Good question. I have no idea."

Footsteps came their way. Was that…?

His pulse raced. It was one of the men. And he was walking right toward them.

Ashley's heartbeat pounded in her ears. Her blood raced through her veins, hot and urgent. What was going on? Why were these men being so brazen?

Christopher stiffened beside her. Had he spotted one of them? She dared not speak, just in case he had. She dared not move or do anything that might give away their whereabouts.

Christopher turned toward her. Even in the dim light, she could sense the urgency in his eyes as he put a finger over his lips to motion "quiet."

"Do you see them?" someone yelled nearby.

"I lost them. They can't be far," another man replied.

"The police are looking for us. We don't have much time."

The second voice got closer. "We shouldn't need much time. They have to be around here somewhere."

"Make it quick."

One of the men muttered profanities under his breath. Ashley could see their legs. The men were right beside the comforter display. Right beside them.

Ashley closed her eyes, lifting up fervent prayers. *Lord, keep us invisible.*

"The police are coming. We've got to go. We'll find them later!"

The men took off in a run.

Her heart stilled…but only for a moment.

They waited what was probably another ten minutes— it felt like hours, though. Finally, when the area was clear of both the shooters and the cops, Christopher nudged the mattress from above them. He stepped out and grabbed her hand, pulling her to her feet.

"Look calm and collected," he whispered.

She nodded, and they casually began walking toward the door. Her gaze scanned the area again. Two officers hovered near the store's mall entrance.

They probably didn't know to look for Christopher and Ashley—yet. All of their efforts were focused on the gunmen. When they reviewed the security tapes later, they'd see Christopher and Ashley fleeing. They'd want to bring them in for questioning.

Still, Christopher grabbed a coat from a rack and handed it to her. "Put this on."

She didn't argue. She slipped the blue coat on over her

white one. Christopher grabbed another coat from across the aisle and did the same.

Smart thinking, just in case anyone was looking for them. They'd be able to slip outside and get away—hopefully.

Christopher dropped some money on the register as they passed.

Finally, they reached the outside doors and stepped into the parking lot. Bright sunlight hit them. Police cars swarmed the building.

An officer reached for them. "You need to get out of the way. There are shooters in the building!"

They nodded and ran toward their SUV. As they passed a police cruiser, a radio crackled inside. "We're looking for a man and a woman also. The woman is wearing a white coat…"

Ashley willed herself to keep her steps casual, to not draw attention to themselves. The SUV was just within sight. Only a few more steps…

When she was within arm's reach, she broke into a jog and climbed inside. Each of her limbs shook with fear, with the mounting pressure of how serious this situation was. Christopher cranked the engine and they took off down the road. At last, they were safe.

For a moment, at least.

# SEVEN

Christopher's thoughts raced as he started down the road. How had those men found them? Christopher's only guess was that they realized Ashley was with him, and that he worked for Eyes. Perhaps they'd had men stationed near the Eyes' headquarters, just waiting for them to leave. But that would take a lot of planning and manpower. Why would they put so many resources toward tracking down and killing Ashley?

"That was a nightmare. A dark, horrific nightmare." Ashley slunk down in the seat and rubbed her temples. "I hope that poor security guard is okay. I hope no one else was hurt."

"Me, too," he muttered.

"I can't even comprehend how someone could do that."

No, she couldn't. That's because she was sweet and innocent. He wouldn't want her to be any other way. But he had to be honest with her.

"Ashley, this is going to be all over the news."

She nodded and nibbled on her thumbnail. "I know."

"The police—maybe even the FBI—are going to pore over all of the security-camera footage from the mall. That could eventually lead them to us. I don't know how long we're going to be able to keep your brother and nephew's disappearance under wraps."

"I'll just push as hard as I can until they track us down. At least I have a head start."

What was she thinking? That if she found her brother and nephew, she'd be able to burst through the doors to save them single-handedly? He was trying to leave the decisions in her hands, for the most part, at least. After all, it was her family that was on the line.

But how far should he let her go? He didn't know. He only knew that he'd be by her side and try to protect her from any danger that came her way. She *was* going to do this with or without him.

He sighed and they headed toward a more upscale area of Virginia Beach, careful to avoid the icy patches on the road. They traveled back toward her brother's house. They had to remain low and not draw any attention to themselves. These men had found them at the mall. Certainly they could find them at her brother's house, an obvious choice for where they might go.

At Ashley's direction, he pulled into a subdivision, a place where no doubt many doctors and lawyers lived— people who earned a nice paycheck. The homes were all brick and large with expansive yards. Each lawn was neatly manicured. Her brother had done well for himself.

"Park here." Ashley pointed to a section of trees.

"On the street?"

She nodded. "Trust me."

The thing was, he did trust her. She had a great head on her shoulders. But this situation…it was hard to know exactly what to do when thrust into an unknown circumstance like this one.

He pulled up along the curb to an area on the edge of the neighborhood. A large cluster of trees stood to one side. Snow and ice frosted the tree limbs and blanketed most of the ground. From the look of those dark clouds in the distance, they'd be getting some more snow soon.

"Did the guys from Eyes check out the place?" she asked.

Christopher nodded. "Yeah, there are two guys stationed outside of the house now. They haven't seen any signs that someone's there. Despite that, we need to play it safe."

Ashley nibbled on her lip as she stared at the woods. "If we cut through those trees, we'll get to my brother's house. His neighbor is out of town for the next week. They're down in Disney World. If we can get into their backyard, they have a massive tree house that offers a bird's-eye view of my brother's yard. We can watch from there to see if anyone is at the house." She glanced at him. "What do you think?"

"It sounds like a place to start. Let me check in with the guys first." He dialed their number. The men were stationed in cars at opposite ends of the house, and there were no new updates since they'd spoken earlier. Christopher told them that they were headed over. Those guards would offer a second set of eyes, but they'd still need to take precautions.

He popped his door open. "Let's go."

She gripped his arm, her touch causing warmth to spread through his veins. In all these years, Ashley hadn't lost her ability to affect him like that. "But they'll see our footprints in the snow."

"We'll see theirs also. That's the good news. I'll find a branch to try and cover up our tracks. The snow didn't make it through all of those tree limbs in the wooded area, though, so that will help."

She stared at him another moment, apprehension knotting between her eyes, before finally nodding and opening her door. He grabbed a branch and began wiping away evidence of their path. His kept his gaze attuned to passing cars or anyone suspicious. He saw no one. Still, he remained on guard. Things weren't always as they seemed. He had firsthand knowledge of that.

They traveled quickly through the patch of trees until finally they reached a privacy fence. He motioned for Ashley to stay back as he crept forward. A gate waited along the back of the barrier.

He tugged at the handle. It was locked. He nodded at Ashley before scaling the fence and unlatching the gate for her. She slipped inside, her breaths coming out in raspy, icy puffs. She pressed herself into the wooden pickets, her wide-eyed gaze soaking in everything around her.

The good news was that he hadn't seen any other footprints or signs that anyone was around. The bad news was that it was biting-cold outside and would only get colder as the sun began to sink farther on the horizon.

He spotted the tree house in the distance. They crept toward the massive, hand-built structure. Ashley climbed the ladder to the top, Christopher right behind her. His gaze continued to scan the area as they moved, waiting for a sign that they had been spotted.

So far, so good.

They scrambled inside. The walls of the tree house blocked the bitter wind that swept over the area—at least a little.

Christopher peered out the window. Ashley was right. This tree house did offer the perfect view of her brother's house and yard. "How'd you know about this tree house? That the family was out of town?"

"I bring David over here to play sometimes."

"You're really close to him, aren't you?"

"Yeah, I love him…like he's my own."

"He's lucky to have you."

She nodded. Why did she look like the motion was painful, though? Why did her gaze look so strained?

He didn't have time to ponder that now. Instead, he watched the backyard. When he'd known Josh, he'd lived in a townhouse in an older part of town. So much had changed in the years since he'd talked to Ashley last.

"It looks like your brother has done well for himself." He kept his gaze on the backyard.

"With a better job and more money, unfortunately, has come less time for the family."

"Nothing's worth sacrificing family." Even as he said the words, he realized how Ashley would probably take them. After all, wasn't that why he'd broken up with her?

She said nothing, so he continued to watch silently. The sun began to sink, cloaking the area in dusky gray, until finally the night was on them.

He'd seen no signs of movement. If they were going to check out the house, now was the time. He looked back at Ashley. "You ready?"

"Ready as I'll ever be."

He reached for her hand. "Let's go, then."

Now, why did he have to reach for her hand? Ashley had been doing just fine sitting huddled in the corner by herself, trying to get his words out of her mind.

*Nothing's worth sacrificing family.*

Nothing except his career, Ashley supposed.

She couldn't let those thoughts linger in her mind, though. They'd only make her weak. Right now, she had to concentrate on finding Josh and David. That was all there was to it.

Christopher pulled her along, his hand warm and strong

and way too familiar. Relief filled her when he released his grip in order to help her jump the fence. A moment later, he landed beside her and they ran toward Josh's house. Christopher covered their tracks again as they moved, making sure no one could easily trace them.

As they climbed onto the deck, Ashley pulled her keys from her pocket. The metal was cold on her already numb fingers—apparently they weren't completely numb, though. She could still feel the bitter cold. Christopher took them from her, calmly inserted them into the back door, and they slipped inside.

They both paused, listening in the dark room. All Ashley could hear was her heartbeat in her ears. Christopher held up a finger to his lips, signaling her to stay quiet and to stay where she was. He crept around the edge of the house and upstairs, making sure everything was clear. Ashley could barely breathe. Around every corner, she waited, expecting someone to jump out.

But there was nothing.

Christopher returned and shoved a flashlight into her hand. Turning on the lights would be too risky, be too obvious of a sign that they were here.

"Where should we start?"

"Let's look on Josh's desk," she whispered. "Maybe there's a clue there." She started toward the corner room on the first floor. Christopher stuck close by. Just having him near calmed her spirit, made her feel like she could face giants.

"You have any idea what we should look for?"

She shook her head, shining her light across the wooden floorboards. "No, but I'm assuming we'll know when we see it."

"Sounds like a good theory to me."

She stepped into the office and scanned the room. Josh's

computer was gone. All three of them. But otherwise, everything appeared in place.

Strange.

She hurried across the room to her brother's desk and shoved some papers aside. There were bills, hand-scribbled notes and piles of paper for his work. There was nothing, however, that gave her any idea of what was going on.

She grabbed his calendar and began flipping through it while Christopher paced the perimeter. "Anything?"

"Not yet," she mumbled. She flipped through the pages. There, on the month of December, was an address. Who's address was that? It was for a place about an hour north of here in Williamsburg.

It might not be anything, but right now it was all she had to go on.

She stuffed his calendar and some other random papers into a backpack. Then she turned toward Christopher. "I think this is as good as it's going to get."

"Come on. Let's get out of here before we test our luck."

Ashley grabbed his arm and pointed to the window. A shadow lingered there. "We may be too late."

Christopher pulled Ashley back, tucking her behind a wall and out of the line of sight for any windows on that side of the house. His gaze darted about the house, looking for signs that anyone else was outside. He saw nothing, but still didn't let down his guard.

Slowly, he pulled out his cell phone. One of the guards outside answered. "Are you both still in your car?" Christopher asked.

"We're still here. Haven't seen any signs of movement out here."

"We think someone is at the back door. It's not one of you?"

"No, sir. We can go check it out."

Christopher clenched his teeth. "Be careful." He hung up and turned back toward Ashley. "How do you feel about guns?"

"If using one is what I have to do, I'll do it."

"Good, because as soon as we get out of here, I'm getting you one."

"My brother has one upstairs under his bed," she whispered.

He raised his eyebrows. "He does?"

She nodded. "I always worried about him having it with David in the house."

"Why would your brother have a gun?"

She shrugged. "I don't know. He said something about everyone having the right to defend their home or something."

"You okay with going up there to get it?" His gaze flickered up the stairs. He hated to separate, but he had to go into this potential battle with every resource possible.

Fear glimmered in her eyes for a moment, but she nodded, anyway. "If it means staying alive to find David then absolutely."

"I'll keep an eye on things down here. Just stay low and stay quiet. No lights."

"Got it."

His throat tightened as he watched her creep toward the staircase. *Please, Lord, watch over her.* He knew there was only one staircase in the home. He'd already checked the upstairs once and found it safe. She should be okay running up there to get the gun and back.

In the meantime, he had to keep his eyes open for the man he'd seen outside the home. Where had he gone? What exactly was he doing?

The men yesterday had annihilated Christopher's house

without hesitation. The person outside the house now was quiet, almost stealthlike in whatever they were doing. Why the change?

Ashley crept back down the stairs. Relief filled him. So far, so good.

She handed him a metal-sided case. Carefully, he opened the box, pulled out the handgun and shoved the magazine in place. "Only put your finger on the trigger when you're ready to shoot," he whispered.

Her hands trembled beneath his, but she nodded. "Got it."

"I want you to stay right here. If someone comes into the house, shoot them."

Her eyes were wide as she nodded.

"I'm going to check out the perimeter. I'll be right back." He locked gazes with her. "Don't come looking for me."

She nodded again.

He stayed low around the edges of the house. He peered out windows but saw no one. Still, his heart pounded in his ears.

His People. They weren't a group to be messed with. How had Josh gotten himself entangled with them? And why did he really have a gun in the house? Josh had never seemed like the gun type, more like the intellectual pacifist. Had something spooked him recently?

After he went around the entire house, he found Ashley again, still pressed against the wall and standing at full attention. "Did you hear anything?"

"Only you." Ashley shivered. "Did they leave?"

"The guys are checking it out right now."

Just then, someone knocked at the door. "Agent Jordan, it's me."

He opened the door, and a rosy-cheeked guard came inside. "There were definitely footprints on the deck. Three sets. We can assume one belonged to you, another to Ms. Wilson and the third to an unknown person. All three sets led through the snow and out the back gate. We didn't catch anyone."

So someone had been here, most likely seen Christopher and Ashley inside, and left. But why?

He leveled his gaze with Ashley. "We've got to go."

She didn't argue. The guard drove them back to their SUV. Christopher checked it out for signs of tampering before they climbed in and locked the doors. A brief moment of relief filled the air. They'd made it this far.

Ashley turned toward him, concern lacing her gaze. "What now?"

He cranked the engine and pulled onto the street. "Now you go back to the Eyes headquarters."

She shook her head. "I have another idea. I want to go to the address I found on my brother's calendar." She glanced at her watch. "It's only six-thirty. It's not too late to show up somewhere unannounced."

"That's not a good idea." It sounded like a terrible idea, for that matter. Best-case scenario, the address was nothing except a random location that had nothing to do with this fiasco. Worst-case scenario, they were walking right into the hands of the men who were trying to kill them.

"Do you have a better one?"

He nodded, his jaw firmly set. "Yeah, I do. Taking you somewhere safe. That's my idea."

She straightened beside him. He couldn't see her gaze, but he imagined the indignation there. "Christopher, this is my problem, not yours. And it doesn't matter where I am. I don't feel safe anywhere right now. I can't just sit around and be passive. I've got to find answers."

"The deeper into this we get, the lesser the chance I can keep you safe."

"I don't want you to keep me safe, Christopher." Her words came out faster and faster.

"Then why did you come to me?" It was a fair question and one that he'd been tossing around since last night.

"Because I need help."

"Why me?" He glanced over to catch a glimpse of her eyes.

Her cheeks flushed and she looked away. "It's complicated."

"I'd say we have time."

She squeezed her lips together and stared in the distance. "I really just want to concentrate on finding Josh and David now. You don't have to come. You can walk away right now if you want to."

He shook his head resolutely. "I'm not walking away." He was in too far. Plus, they still didn't have that closure he'd hoped for.

"Don't say I didn't offer."

"By the end of this, I want an answer from you. I want an explanation, Ashley, on why you came to me, of all people. I think I at least deserve that."

She nodded, her features strained.

He started driving toward the address.

# EIGHT

As they continued down the road, Ashley's chest felt like a gigantic brick pressed on it. She had to tell Christopher the truth sometime. But she dreaded how he would take the news.

In her mind, she'd tried to remember Christopher as someone who was so career-focused that he was heartless. But seeing him again, she knew that wasn't true. He would have been a great father—loving in discipline, gentle in teaching and active in life.

Guilt pressed in on her.

If only things had been different. A million times she had questioned her decision on giving up David for adoption. Maybe she should have kept him, gotten some kind of job that didn't take a college degree and become a single mom.

But she'd wanted her boy to have a stable home life, one with a mom and a dad. She didn't want him to face the uncertainty of whether or not they'd have electricity or groceries. Nor had she wanted to depend on the government or her parents.

Then she'd been in the car accident and had spent six months in the hospital trying to recover. Her brother had taken care of her baby in the process. When she saw how her brother and his wife had bonded with David, she knew what she had to do. She'd prayed about the decision and had peace when she decided to see if her brother wanted to adopt. Right now that choice seemed like the worst idea ever, though.

"What are you thinking about?"

Christopher's voice pulled her out of her churning thoughts. She shrugged. "Not much." Yet the truth was that she'd been thinking about everything.

Did Christopher need to know about David? Did he *really* need to know? Maybe it would be better if she spared him the truth. But could she live with herself if she did?

The lines used to seem so clear to her, but they no longer were.

"My GPS is saying we're almost there. This look familiar to you at all?"

They'd headed north from Virginia Beach toward Williamsburg. They'd pulled off the interstate thirty minutes ago and were now traveling on the dark, snow-slicked back roads of the community. Occasionally they passed a store or a house, but mostly they passed trees.

"No, this doesn't seem familiar."

Finally, they pulled into a neighborhood full of large, brick townhomes. Ashley looked at the address again and pointed. "Right there."

Christopher pulled to a stop in front of the house. Two windows were lit, making it appear that someone was home. Ashley's hand went to the door handle, but Christopher's kept her in the car. She looked back at him. He'd gone from casual to all business in a matter of seconds. His eyes left no room for argument.

"Be careful. If anything happens to me, run."

His words caused an ominous dread to form in her gut.

Despite that, she opened her door. Her feet hit the crunchy snow that had been packed down by passing cars. She shook off any fear that threatened to grasp her and fell into step beside Christopher.

She paused by the car parked in the short driveway as they passed it. Why did the vehicle look familiar? It was a burgundy luxury sedan. She shook her head, unable to place it at the moment.

They reached the porch. Christopher directed her to stand to the side as he knocked. Ashley could see the tension in his shoulders, in the set of his jaw. Would this be another ambush attack? Would the next sound they heard be that of gunfire?

*Lord, watch over us.*

She'd been praying that prayer a lot lately. John 14:27 flittered through her mind. "Let not your hearts be troubled, neither let them be afraid."

*Lord, I'm failing at that command. Forgive me. Help me.*

A moment later, someone pulled the door open. Quiet stretched for a moment. Ashley would take that over the sound of an automatic weapon. Still, she willed herself to remain to the side, out of the line of sight.

"Can I help you?" A masculine voice came from inside the house. Why did it sound familiar, like she'd heard it before?

"We'd like to ask you a few questions," Christopher started.

"Me? Why would you want to ask me any questions? And who are you?"

She dared to glance over and satisfy her curiosity. She blinked at the figure she saw there. "Wally?" She stepped from the shadows.

Wally Stancil's eyes widened beneath his oversize

glasses. He stood only a few inches taller than her five feet, six inches. His thinness only added to his small demeanor. "Ashley Wilson? What are you doing here? It's been a while."

She shook her head, disbelief filling her. "I had no idea this was your house."

"And I had no idea you'd show up here."

"You guys know each other?" Christopher asked, slight annoyance across his face. "Can someone fill me in?"

Ashley pointed to the man at the door. "Wally is one of my brother's coworkers."

"Don't forget to mention that we did go out on a date once also," he added, his eyes sparkling as he pushed his glasses up higher on his nose.

Ashley forced a smile. It had been one of the worst dates of her life. They'd had absolutely no chemistry, but she couldn't quite convince Wally of that. Her lips twisted in a half smile. "Wally, this is an old friend, Christopher Jordan."

"Nice to meet you." He waved his hand toward the inside of the house. "Get out of the cold. Come in and tell me what I can do to help you."

Ashley stepped inside, Christopher close behind. Wally led them to a living room off the entryway and offered them some coffee, which they both refused. Finally, they all settled across from each other on couches that faced each other. Wally flipped off the TV, where news coverage of the mall shooting was on.

Wally pointed to the screen. "Did you hear about that? Some rough stuff. Not sure what's happening in this world."

Ashley's throat burned. "I heard. It's just terrible. Did they catch the guys who did it yet?"

He shook his head. "Not yet. They're not sure how

they disappeared. I guess there are four persons of interest all together. Three men and one woman. That's all they're saying."

"Scary," Ashley muttered. She knew firsthand just how scary it was.

"Now, to what do I owe the pleasure of this visit?" Wally leaned toward them, curiosity showing in his eyes. "I don't suppose you're here to beg me to go out with you again?"

Ashley smiled apologetically. "I'm actually trying to find out some information on my brother."

His eyebrows shot up. "Your brother? Josh? What about him?"

She licked her lips, trying to figure out how to approach the subject delicately. "I know the two of you work together. I was hoping you could tell me if he's been acting strangely lately."

Wally shrugged. "Not that I can think of. Is he okay? I noticed he didn't come into work yesterday. I assumed he wasn't feeling well."

"That's what we're trying to figure out," Christopher said. "Anything you might know would be helpful."

Wally's gaze flickered back and forth momentarily before he shook his head. "I'm afraid I can't help. I know he's been busy lately. We haven't had much time to talk."

Ashley wasn't ready to give up. "I saw your address was on his calendar. It looked like you'd gotten together recently."

Wally shifted in his seat but remained composed and calm. "We talked about getting together, but he canceled on me at the last minute. He said there was something he wanted to discuss, something about work. I never found out what it was."

Ashley leaned closer. "And you have no idea?"

He shook his head again. "No, I have no idea."

"Exactly what kind of project was he working on at TechShare?" Christopher asked.

"What kind of project?" He drew in a deep breath. "We were just doing some programming for a new computer processor the company is trying to develop. Nothing exciting."

"Is the new processor something that other companies were trying to get their hands on?" Christopher asked.

Wally shrugged. "I suppose the product was competitive. I mean, technology changes so fast. Every company wants to be at the top of their game. TechShare is no different. We hadn't been warned about any direct threats, however."

"Is there someone at the job who could speak directly to the matter?" Christopher asked.

Wally's bony shoulders again reached toward the ceiling. "I guess you could call our boss." He grabbed some paper from the table and jotted something down. "Here's his number."

Ashley took the paper and slipped it into her pocket as another thought formed in her mind. She raised her chin and glanced at Wally. "I have a better idea. Maybe I'll visit him in the office."

He shook his head. "They don't really smile on unexpected visitors."

"We'll handle that. In the meantime, what's the address?" Christopher pressed.

Wally's gaze moved back and forth between the two of them. Finally, he snatched the paper back and jotted down something else. "Don't say I didn't warn you."

Ashley didn't know what that meant, but she nodded, anyway. They all stood, and Wally walked them toward the door. She wished she'd found more answers, but at least they had somewhere to go from here.

Streetlights flickered by, momentarily lighting the interior of the SUV, as they left the dark neighborhood. Ashley's thoughts turned over and over, trying to make sense of things, trying to find answers that were just out of her reach.

"So you really went on a date with that guy?"

She pulled her lips into a tight line. "I did. There was a lot of pressure from my family. They kept spouting something about me having expectations that are too high."

"So they wanted you to settle?"

"Exactly." She'd grumbled about that very thing on many occasions, but no one seemed to understand her. "I went out with Wally just to appease them. But it was a horrible date. We had nothing to talk about. Nothing in common. And I couldn't even fake being interested in our conversation or our food or anything, really." The truth was: no one could compare to Christopher. She'd been on a lot of dates, but no one measured up.

"He certainly seemed happy to see you."

Her lips pulled tighter.

"And he's certainly the opposite of me. Maybe you should give him another chance. Maybe he's exactly what you need."

She scowled at him. "You're funny. At least you think you are."

"Come on, Ashley—"

She softened her voice. "I'm not the same person I used to be, Christopher. Life happens. You change. Things you used to like, you don't like anymore." Things like tough military men with soft hearts. *Like you.*

His expression sobered. "You're right. People do change."

And with people changing, relationships changed. *Like us, for example. Why did I ever think we would work together?* The idea was crazy.

At one time, she'd thought they were perfect together. But now she realized that she craved someone who'd be home every night, someone with a job that didn't put his life on the line. Most of all, she craved being with someone who'd make her feel loved. All Christopher had done was make her realize that she hadn't been worth it to him.

She crossed her arms over her chest. "So what now? Talking to Wally didn't give us any more answers. I still have no idea why my brother and nephew would be snatched or where they might be or what to do next."

"You've got to give it more time."

"I don't have more time! With every minute that passes, I feel like my brother and nephew are that much farther out of reach." She hated that her voice rose with each word; she hated the despair that crept into her inflection.

Christopher's gaze landed on her. "Maybe we should call the authorities in, Ashley. They are more well-equipped to handle these things. Besides, they're probably looking for us after that debacle at the mall."

She shook her head. "I can't. They made it clear that they'd kill David and Josh if I reported what happened."

"That doesn't make sense. They're keeping them alive for a reason. Otherwise, they would have just shot them on the spot. They've got to know the authorities are going to find out at some point. Josh won't show up for work. His mail won't be collected. David won't be at school. Whether you tell them or not, eventually the police are going to figure out something is wrong."

Ashley bit down on her lip. He was right. So why had

they threatened her not to tell? Was it because she could describe them? Had they been trying to buy more time?

They did want her brother and nephew alive, she realized. That was the good news.

The bad news was that they wanted her dead. Or were they trying to abduct her also? Nothing made sense.

Was it possible that this nightmare had only taken place over two days' time? It felt like weeks had passed since she saw Josh and David abducted.

He pulled into a parking lot. "Here's the office." He glanced at the address again. "It's a bit smaller than I imagined. You ever been here before?"

Ashley shook her head. "No, I haven't. I doubt anyone's here. All the lights are off."

"We might as well knock since we're here." He glanced at her. "You stay here in the SUV. Lock the doors behind me. And keep that gun handy. Got it?"

She nodded.

She watched as Christopher approached the dark glass door. She realized probably no one was here, but they had to try, anyway. At least it was something.

He knocked at the door, his gaze constantly roving the area. The darkness surrounding them made Ashley shiver. A lone light lit the parking lot and the blue letters from TechShare offered a slight glow. But regardless, she felt so isolated out here, like anyone could get to them.

Just like they'd done today at the mall.

She shivered again as she thought about it.

Christopher climbed back into the SUV. "No one's there. We'll have to try again on Monday. Maybe we can figure out something then."

The long day was beginning to pull at her. She was tired, both physically and emotionally.

"I say we go back to Eyes and report to Jack and Denton everything that's happened today."

She nodded and put her head into the seat.

*Let not your hearts be troubled, neither let them be afraid.*

That verse was going to be harder to implement than she'd like.

# NINE

As soon as they arrived back at the Eyes headquarters, Christopher suggested they grab a bite to eat since food had been the last thing on either of their minds throughout the day. The cafeteria employees were gone, but he was able to pull together some leftovers from an earlier meal.

They sat across from each other in the cafeteria with stewed beef served in crusty bread bowls. Both ate silently for several minutes. Outside, darkness stared at them. It reminded him a bit of his past and his future. His past was filled with bad memories; the future was filled with uncertainties.

He watched Ashley a moment, wondering what was going through her mind. He wished he could reach out to her more, but he couldn't. It wasn't his place. He'd simply help her to work through this whole ordeal on her own time. What else could he do?

"What would you be doing now if I hadn't shown up at your doorstep?" Ashley asked, tearing off a piece of bread.

"I'd be working around the house probably." Trying to touch that ever-elusive thing called peace. He took another bite of his stew, savoring the warmth, as well as the quiet around him. "As you could probably tell by the boxes scattered around everywhere, it was a work in progress."

She frowned. "I'll pay you back for any damages there. I know it's a mess."

He waved her off. "I'm not worried about it." He wiped his mouth. "How about you, Ashley? What would you be doing on an ordinary weekend?"

She looked off into the distance, as if entering a different world for a moment. "I would have probably stopped by to see if David wanted to play in the snow with me." A faint smile brushed her lips. "He loves the snow, and we don't always get a lot of it around here."

"It sounds like you're really close to him." Every time she said his name, her voice became warmer and her eyes softer.

She nodded. "I am. Josh's job consumes him sometimes, so I spend a lot of time with David. It's especially nice because I work at home, so my schedule is flexible. I even have a bedroom set up for David at my condo."

"I always knew you'd be a great mom."

Her face lost its color. "What?"

He shrugged. "You know, you're great with kids. I know you don't have any of your own, but you'd probably get the award for being Super Aunt or something."

She laughed weakly and muttered, "Thanks."

"You live in Virginia Beach?"

She shook her head. "Portsmouth. Only a block from the Elizabeth River, close to the downtown area. It's kind of fun to be able to walk places."

She'd always been idealistic, wanting to live in a small town where everyone knew everyone. They'd talked about moving out to the mountains one day, out toward where there was a slower pace of life. "And your dad?"

"He's down in South Carolina now, living in one of those retirement communities. He plays golf every day.

He loves it. I even think he might be *dating* a widow he met there."

"I heard about your mom's passing. I'm sorry about that." A mutual friend had shared the news, but he hadn't wanted to complicate anything by calling Ashley to offer his sympathy. They'd only been broken up a few months at the time.

"It was a shock to all of us. It's amazing how life can change in the blink of an eye. First it was my mom from a heart attack. Six years later, Lena died of cancer. Now Josh and David have been abducted. It seems surreal." She shook her head in disbelief before clearing her throat. "How about you? How's your family?"

"My granddad passed away three years ago. You probably figured that out when we were at his house." He'd left the place to Christopher, but it wasn't the same without his granddad there. Still, he'd hold those memories close, and being at the house was the easiest place to do that.

"He was a good man."

"He was," Christopher agreed. "My mom got remarried and moved to Maine. She seems really happy. I haven't talked to my dad in years. I think I was ten the last time he popped into my life. Then there's me."

"You've been back for three months you said?"

He nodded. "That's right. I'm still trying to adjust to life back here in the commonwealth." He was trying to adjust to life, period. Everything about his psyche felt so rocky right now. Would he ever be in a place where he was ready for a relationship, where he felt capable of opening himself up? Sometimes—most of the time—he felt like the answer was clearly a "no." Some of his friends had returned from war without an arm or a leg. Christopher had returned with what felt like part of his soul missing, forever lost on those deadly battlegrounds and amidst the horror of war.

"I thought for sure that you'd be career military. I just can't get over the fact that you're back here."

"As someone told me earlier today, people change."

Her eyes quickly lit with amusement before fading into a dull shimmer. "Yes, they do."

He leaned toward her, hungry to find out what she was concealing behind those beautiful eyes of hers. "But the core of a person stays the same, don't you think?"

She shrugged, her gaze fluttering up to meet his. "Maybe."

"Take you, for example. You're still Ashley Wilson. You still have a great smile. You're still smart and athletic and you care about others. Maybe your experiences have changed. Maybe your views have changed. But you're still Ashley."

"Life is always a process, isn't it? If I stayed the same and stayed sheltered from all the storms, I wouldn't appreciate life nearly as much as I do today." She leaned closer. "How about you? You're obviously still tough and protective. What's changed about you?"

Himself. Now that was a topic he wasn't ready to talk about. He leaned back as memories began to crowd in again. "War's changed me, Ashley. I've seen too many things. Too much death. Too much hurt."

War had damaged him too much, so much that he knew he'd been broken beyond repair. His future seemed bleak, like any possibility of a healthy relationship was gone. He'd seen and experienced a great deal of tragedy.

She leaned back and bit her lip for a moment, sweet

compassion staining her gaze. "I can't imagine being in your shoes."

"I'm glad you've never been in my shoes. They haven't always been fun shoes to wear." His footsteps included dragging the lifeless body of his best friend back to the Humvee, rushing him back to camp in the hope the medics there could save him.

They couldn't.

There had been too much death. Too much pain. Too much loss.

She cleared her throat and whispered, "For what it's worth, I appreciate everyone who's served the country like you have."

Her words did warm his heart for a moment. It had taken her a lot of strength to say that, especially since his service to the country had led him away from her. "Thank you."

She nodded. "No, thank you." She stared at her half-eaten food for a moment before letting out a long sigh. "If it's okay, I'm going to turn in for the night."

"There's a church service here on the campus tomorrow morning at nine. You interested?"

"Yeah, that sounds great. I'll meet you in the hallway at 8:45? Does that work?"

"Sounds great. See you then." He watched her walk away.

Maybe they were making some progress in mending the divides in their relationship. Sometimes, out of the most devastating circumstances, the most beautiful things could grow. He remembered that flower garden on the base in Afghanistan again.

He hoped forgiveness might bloom out of the horrific circumstances surrounding them now.

Good memories, he reminded himself. Out of all the bad, he was going to walk away from this with something good.

The church service the next morning had been held in a small chapel located on the lower level of the Eyes' main building or "The Lodge" as Ashley had heard it called. According to Christopher, they'd hired a chaplain and began services there a few months ago. Some of their trainees stayed at the facilities for a couple of weeks at a time. They'd found the chapel to be an optimal place of comfort and spiritual "training."

The service had been nice and brought back some of Ashley's focus. She could always tell when her faith began to waver because her life felt scattered, her worries felt greater and regrets haunted her. But when she read God's word and focused on trusting Him, all the little stuff in life seemed to fall into place. Even if it didn't, she felt like she had the strength to handle it.

And her brother and David's abduction was no small thing, but she was still praying for wisdom.

After the service, she and Christopher had lunch in the cafeteria with Jack and his wife, as well as several other people who worked at Eyes. The cook had whipped up spaghetti and meatballs, and the savory scent filled her with a yearning for home. Instead, she tried to enjoy the people around her.

Jack's wife, Rachel, ran a nonprofit called 26 Letters, which set up volunteers to write letters to members of the military stationed overseas. She had a son named Aidan who looked around seven years old and the bump on her abdomen hinted that a new baby might be coming in a few months.

Every time Ashley looked at the boy, she was reminded of David, and sadness pressed on her heart.

She wished she could enjoy the conversation, that she could forget about the problems at hand and simply focus on being social.

But she couldn't do it.

First her thoughts drifted to how nice it would be to be a part of such a group. Then she thought about how nice it would be just to be a part of a couple. What would it be like to have someone to share her secrets with? Someone to help her carry her burdens? Someone to tell her everything would be okay?

But all those thoughts weren't getting her any closer to finding two of the people she loved the most in this world.

Finally, she leaned over and whispered to Christopher, "Do you think it would be okay if I used a computer?"

He wiped his mouth before nodding. "I can arrange that. We have secure lines up in my office. Even your brother couldn't hack into their systems."

"You don't think so? He's brilliant."

He stood and placed his napkin in his seat. "Didn't he get in trouble in high school for that?"

Her cheeks reddened as she also stood. "Yeah, he got bored and hacked into the school system's servers and changed some grades," she whispered, hoping no one else heard. "That doesn't mean anything."

He raised his hands. "I wasn't accusing anyone. I'm just trying to put the pieces together."

She forced a smile at the crowd of people at the table now staring at them. She offered a small wave. "Nice to meet all of you. Thanks for letting me eat with you."

They all called out their goodbyes. They really were a nice group. What would it be like to chat with them outside of this situation? It didn't matter because that was never going to happen.

Christopher led her upstairs to his office, a plain space with no decorations or personal touches. The room could have been anyone's office. She shook her head for a moment. "You need to put up a few pictures or something in here. It looks depressing."

He grinned at her. "Decorating isn't exactly my first priority, but I'll keep that in mind."

Yes, he could use a woman's touch. But not her touch. Someone else's. Maybe one of those nice women downstairs had a friend they could set him up with.

Despite how Ashley tried to be nonchalant with her thoughts, her heart still tugged with…something. What was that? Longing? Attraction?

Those were emotions she needed to shove way, way down until they disappeared, never to be found again.

He glanced up at her, his eyes twinkling for a moment, as he pulled up the computer screen. Perhaps she'd overstepped her boundaries and been too personal with him. She should have kept things simple and professional.

He stepped back. "The computer's all yours."

She settled in the chair and typed in the web address for her email server. She wanted to make sure her brother hadn't tried to contact her. Christopher continued to stand beside her, his arms crossed as if he was on guard against her doing something stupid.

She glanced up at him. "I just want to check my email."

"Do you really think your brother emailed you?"

She shook her head. "No, but if anyone's trying to contact me, this is how they'll do it. I'm constantly on my computer emailing people, both for personal and professional purposes. I have some design jobs I'm working on."

"Who hires you?"

She shrugged. "It varies. But my brother helped me develop this security system for my websites. Because of that system, some big companies have hired me instead of doing their websites in house. I've had credit unions, stores, even a pharmaceutical company hire me to do their sites."

"So you're pretty good at this computer stuff yourself."

She shrugged again. "To an extent. Not like my brother. I really like the creative side of it. He likes the technical side."

She glanced up and saw Christopher's eyes were shining with…what was that? Admiration?

Her cheeks flushed, and she looked away. She had to concentrate on the task at hand. Why was she tempted, just for a moment, to concentrate on Christopher, instead?

Because concentrating on Christopher was a bad, bad idea.

Christopher couldn't help but feel a surge of respect for Ashley. She'd risen above some challenging circumstances and been able to achieve her dreams. She'd always been a whiz at graphic design. Not only had she found a career in the field, but she'd excelled. Who wouldn't admire that?

What he still couldn't figure out was why she'd come to him. Of all the people in the world she could have looked to for help, he had no idea why she'd chosen him.

Not that he was complaining. He saw this as a second chance to make things right and not in a "get back together" kind of way. No, he knew there was no chance of that. Even if Ashley could forgive him, the war had left him too broken. But maybe he could make it so she didn't hate him anymore.

He'd given up trying to explain himself and his decisions. He'd given up thinking that she might understand.

They'd been young and in love. They'd never had any disagreements or arguments. They were perfect together. So he could understand that she was hurt over his decision, even if he was trying to do what was best for his country.

"Interesting…" She leaned toward the computer, a wrinkle forming on the skin between her eyes.

He scooted his seat around beside her. "What is it?"

She pointed to an email on the screen. "I don't recognize this email address. The subject line says, 'Urgent.' Normally I'd delete something like that, but with everything that's happened…"

He reached over and clicked on the email for her. A video message popped onto the screen. A boy with light brown hair, freckles and a defined jawline stared at the camera for a moment. Something about the boy seemed familiar…but what?

Ashley gasped beside him. "It's David. That's David."

"Hi, Ashley," his voice rang out. He smiled and did a quick little wave at the camera. A white wall made up the background and nothing else was visible. "My dad's friends told me to make this video for you. They said I should tell you to be quiet. I told them that didn't sound very nice, but they told me to say it, anyway. I miss you. I wish you could come visit—"

Someone cut him off and his image froze on the screen.

Ashley let out a small cry. Christopher squeezed her shoulder, knowing he could never fully comprehend all of the emotions she must be feeling. That boy was like a son to her.

"The good news is that he's okay," he murmured. "He doesn't even look scared."

She nodded, rubbing her lips with her fingers and staring at David's frozen picture on the screen. "That is good news. Why did he say *my dad's friends,* though?"

"That's probably what they told him to say." He leaned closer, squinting at the image on the screen. It looked pretty clean; it was unlikely they'd find clues there. "We need to have this video analyzed, see if technicians can pick up anything."

She nodded, her hand now in a fist over her mouth. She tore her eyes away from the screen long enough to glance at him. "He's so precious, Christopher."

"He looks like one tough, smart kid. Polite, too."

Unreadable emotion flooded her gaze. "You would love him, Christopher. He's great. Adventurous. He's got a bit of a daredevil in him."

He smiled. "It sounds like I would like him. I can't wait to meet him one day."

Tears glimmered in her eyes as she looked away. "I hope you can."

He squeezed her shoulder again. "I will. We're going to get David and your brother back."

She closed her eyes as if trying to conceal her pain. "Thanks."

"I'm going to go get one of our technicians. You stay put here for a moment. Okay?"

"Got it."

Christopher jogged down the hall and grabbed two of the guys who worked IT for them. Adrenaline pumped through his blood as he hurried back toward Ashley. He stepped inside his office in time to see her running her finger down the computer screen. The image made his heart lurch.

She dropped her hand and scooted out of the way as the IT guys surrounded the computer.

"I feel like if I look away then I'm abandoning him," she whispered. "That video's all I have to hold on to right now."

"At least you know he's okay. That's important."

She nodded.

"Let's see what we can find out," one of the technicians started. He pulled his seat closer to the table. "Maybe we can isolate some background noises that will give us some kind of indication as to where they are."

He began typing furiously on the computer's mainframe. He hit a few more keys and scrunched his eyebrows together before sitting back and letting out a grunt.

"What's going on?" Christopher stepped closer and saw that the computer screen had become pixelated.

"Unplug it!" Ashley yelled.

The technician's hands scrambled around the computer until he reached the back and jerked out a wire. He muttered under his breath as the screen finally went black.

Christopher didn't have to ask. He knew what had just happened. A virus. There had been a virus in that email.

These men were trying to get at them at whatever angle they could. He had a feeling Ashley's heart had just been ripped out from her, similar to that computer cable. He had to get to the bottom of this before these people became like a virus to Ashley's soul.

# TEN

Ashley should have known. So much for getting clues there.

But where did that leave them?

She sat on the floor, leaning against the wall of Christopher's office. Her head felt like it weighed a hundred pounds—a hundred throbbing pounds.

When would they ever catch a break? What was she missing?

A hand clamped down on her shoulder. "There will be more clues. Just wait." She looked up and saw Christopher looking down on her.

"That just seemed to be our best one."

With his fingers gently pressing on her arm, he pulled her up. "Come on. Let's let these guys work. There's something I want to do with you."

They started walking toward the other end of the building. "Where are we going?"

He smiled. "You'll see. Grab your coat and gun."

She stopped by her room and did just that before meeting Christopher in the hallway. They walked outside, across the lawn and to another building.

Once she stepped inside, the smell of smoke hit her—

**W**e'd like to send you two free books to introduce you to the Love Inspired® Suspense series. Your two books have a combined cover price of $11.98 or more in the U.S. and $13.50 or more in Canada, but they are yours free! We'll even send you two wonderful surprise gifts. You can't lose!

Each of your **FREE** books is filled with riveting inspiration suspense featurin Christian charact facing challenge to their faith.... and their lives

# GET 2 FREE BOOKS!

## HURRY!
Return this card today to get 2 FREE Books and 2 FREE Bonus Gifts!

*Love Inspired*
## SUSPENSE
RIVETING INSPIRATIONAL ROMANCE

**YES!** Please send me the 2 FREE Love Inspired® Suspense books and 2 free gifts for which I qualify. I understand that I am under no obligation to purchase anything further, as explained on the back of this card.

affix free books sticker here

❏ I prefer the regular-print edition
**123/323 IDL F5FH**

❏ I prefer the larger-print edition
**110/310 IDL F5FH**

*Please Print*

FIRST NAME

LAST NAME

ADDRESS

APT.#          CITY

STATE/PROV.          ZIP/POSTAL CODE

Offer limited to one per household and not applicable to series that subscriber is currently receiving.

**Your Privacy**—The Harlequin® Reader Service is committed to protecting your privacy. Our Privacy Policy is available online at www.ReaderService.com or upon request from the Harlequin Reader Service. We make a portion of our mailing list available to reputable third parties that offer products we believe may interest you. If you prefer that we not exchange your name with third parties, or if you wish to clarify or modify your communication preferences, please visit us at www.ReaderService.com/consumerchoice or write to us at Harlequin Reader Service Preference Service, P.O. Box 9062, Buffalo, NY 14269. Include your complete name and address.

LIS-11/13-LA-13    © 2012 HARLEQUIN ENTERPRISES LIMITED    Printed in the U.S.A.

▼ DETACH AND MAIL CARD TODAY! ▼

only it wasn't the smell of burning wood or metal. This was different, unique in and of itself.

It smelled like the inside of Christopher's house after those men had destroyed it.

It smelled like gunpowder.

She glanced up at Christopher. He grinned, all lopsided and boylike, an image that sent her back in time. "A shooting range," he explained. "It's time to teach you how to handle a gun."

"Is this really necessary?" Certainly, she wouldn't need to use a gun. Except that she knew she might, whether she wanted to or not.

"It could mean the difference of getting your nephew back or not."

She nodded, the decision firmly made up in her mind. "Let's do it then."

The range was empty of anyone but them. He led her to a lane and handed her some earplugs and protective glasses. Then he put the gun she'd retrieved from her room in her hands. The metal felt cold and foreign. But she was willing to take on something new. She didn't have much of a choice.

"Hold you arms out like this," he said, adjusting her reach. "Don't lock your elbows in place."

She loosened her arms, which was the opposite of what she wanted to do. "Got it."

He patted her hip. "Keep your legs shoulder-width apart. There's a bit of a kickback after you fire. Having a steady stance will give you more stability. Just be aware that it's going to happen, though, okay?"

She nodded, wishing he wasn't so close. But he stood right beside her, his arms easily wrapping around her. Not in a romantic way, simply as an instructor and student.

That didn't stop every inch of her skin from becoming alive, however.

"Now, just take your time and aim at the target. Use your dominant eye."

The gun shook in her hands as she held it and pointed toward the target at the end of the berm.

"When you've got your target in sight, press the trigger, don't pull it. That motion keeps you in control."

She could hardly do anything with Christopher standing this close. Nonetheless, she tried to concentrate on what he was saying. Even after all of these years, he still had that effect on her. It was a good thing she'd realized that warm, happy feelings didn't equate into lasting love—even temporary infatuation, for that matter. They usually translated into heartbreak.

Her heart leaped into her throat as she stared down the barrel of the gun. Finally, she pressed the trigger. The kickback took her breath away for a moment, causing a surge of adrenaline. She pulled up her protective eyewear and looked at the target at the end.

Christopher pushed a button and the punctured paper traveled down the ceiling toward them. He studied it a moment before nodding beside her. "Not bad."

She hit a couple of inches north of the center. "What do you know? Maybe I should consider a career change."

He offered a wry grin. "I don't know about that. We need people in the world who have big hearts, and we need people in the world who are ready to jump into battle."

"Didn't you always say that a good SEAL had both of those things?"

He glanced down for a moment. "I might have said that. It takes all kinds of people to make the world go round, right?"

"Sure enough."

His face lost the moment of vulnerability it had presented briefly. He motioned toward the target and his lips pulled tight. "Let's keep working."

What was that about? If Ashley asked, she had a feeling he wouldn't tell her.

They continued to shoot, each round getting better and better. The gun was beginning to feel less foreign and more familiar. Still, she prayed she never had to use it.

Finally, she handed the weapon to him. "Let's see what you can do."

He took the gun from her and began firing. Every shot hit the target dead-on. She was stunned by his accuracy. "I'm impressed."

"You should be. He was the best shooter the military had," someone said behind them.

Ashley looked up as Denton walked into the range. It seemed like every time she saw the man, he brought bad news. Still, she nodded hello.

He stopped in front of her. "Could I chat with you a moment, Ashley?"

Dread filled her. "Of course."

He dipped his head toward the front door. "How about we take a walk? The sidewalks have been cleared enough that they shouldn't be slick."

"Sure thing." She grabbed her coat and pulled it on as she walked toward the exit. As they stepped outside, lemonade-colored sunshine hit them—it felt more like frozen lemonade with the brisk chill in the air, though. Thankfully, the day was warmer than yesterday, even though snow still lingered on the ground.

They began walking silently down the sidewalk. Anticipation built in her as she waited for what Denton had to say. His hands were shoved down into the pockets of his black leather coat, and he walked with slow, purposeful steps.

Finally, he broke the silence. "So I did some research on the boy your brother adopted."

Her cheeks heated, even though she willed them to stop. "Did you?"

"I saw your name listed as the boy's mother."

She dragged her steps for a moment. Did she deny it? Own up to it? More of her carefully controlled life began to crumble. Finally, she nodded. "It's true. I was young and in college—I couldn't support a child. My brother wanted a baby, so he adopted mine. It just all made sense."

Denton glanced over at her. "And the boy's father? Is he in the picture?"

Her throat burned. "I didn't tell him so, no, he's not involved."

His eyebrows shot up. "You didn't tell him?"

Did Denton know? Ashley couldn't be sure. She only knew her heart squeezed with anxiety. "It's a long story. But let's just say when the boy's father left, he made it clear that he wasn't a family man. This was the best choice for all of us."

He nodded. "I see. That's pretty harsh." They took a few more ambling steps. "I guess this is all a secret?"

"You could say that."

"Is there anybody in your past who could want to hurt the boy?"

She pointed her finger at herself. "In *my* past? No, I have nothing to do with this."

"Are you sure?"

"I'm positive. No one knows…"

"You're sure the dad's not a part of this?"

She stopped. "Of course he's not. His name isn't even on the birth certificate."

"I'm asking because if his dad just happened to be on some specially trained team that, let's say, took down terrorists, then that might be another possibility as to why Josh and David were abducted. It could help us to track down the men behind this."

Her cheeks burned as dreadful possibilities filled her. "I don't know what you're talking about." But her mind raced…could that be the connection they were missing?

"Really? Because that boy had the greenest eyes. They almost looked like…" He stopped and shook his head purposefully. "No, I don't know what I'm thinking."

She said nothing. She couldn't say it, couldn't admit it. Or could she? No, this had nothing to do with Christopher. The idea was crazy.

They started walking silently together again. Finally, Denton spoke. "Did Christopher ever tell you what his nickname was as a SEAL?"

She shook her head. She had no idea, and, at the moment, she couldn't even say she really cared.

"They called him Captain America."

Her gaze flicked up toward Denton. "Like the superhero?"

Denton nodded. "Yeah, like the superhero. He was selfless, always trying to look out for everyone else, always talking about how our country was worth fighting for. He was a real inspiration."

"Selfless?" she practically stuttered. A selfless person didn't leave his fiancée six months before the wedding so he could be a better soldier. She bit down and said nothing else.

Denton stared at her a moment before nodding toward the inside. "I guess it's time to get out of the cold."

He started walking away when Ashley grabbed his arm.

"You can't tell anyone about what you found out, Denton. Please. It's…important to me."

Perceptive, compassionate eyes met hers. "It's yours to tell, Ashley. Not mine. But if there's anything else you can tell me that might shine some more light on your brother and nephew's disappearance, please let me know. Nothing is insignificant."

Anxiety and dread pooled in her stomach as she nodded. "Got it."

She stood outside and raised her head toward the wind, letting it hit her skin until she couldn't feel her face anymore. This discomfort beat that of breaking the news to Christopher.

She had to tell him, didn't she? She couldn't put it off any longer.

Christopher shot a few more rounds after Ashley and Denton left the range. Each pull of the trigger seemed to be a release of emotion as doubt and suspicion rose in him.

He lowered his gun and shook his head. What had that been about? What could Denton have wanted to talk privately with Ashley about? He'd put his life on hold to help her, and now she was keeping secrets?

He pulled off his protective eyewear and his earplugs, his thoughts still churning. If he was supposed to know about their conversation, Denton or Ashley would tell him. They wouldn't keep something from him that could be pivotal to their search.

Why didn't that realization make him feel better, though? What was so secretive that he couldn't know, especially when considering everything they'd already been through together? That was the reason he was so up in arms, wasn't it? It had nothing to do with the sparks of electricity he'd felt when he'd taught Ashley to shoot. It had nothing to do with the way her smile was beginning to occupy his thoughts. Because those things, while enjoyable, were off-limits on so many levels.

He tried to brush off those thoughts as he began cleaning his gun. His work here was done. He'd go check on the IT guys and see if they'd found out anything else. At least that quest for information would keep his mind occupied.

As he stepped outside to go back to the main building, he made a mental list of what they needed to do. They needed to visit TechShare again. And then what? Did they have any other leads?

Here in the States, working as a civilian, they didn't have satellite surveillance or intelligence like he'd had when he was a SEAL. Here, he had to rely on good old-fashioned investigating if he wanted to find any answers.

He paused when he saw Ashley standing on the sidewalk, her face raised to the wind and eyes squeezed shut as if in agony. What was going on?

And why did she have to look so beautiful, even in her distressed state? She still had the ability to take his breath away. There wasn't a single thing about her that wasn't lovely and loveable, all the way from her pert nose and glossy hair to her fiercely loyal spirit and warm gaze.

She opened her eyes and caught him staring at her. She quickly straightened but didn't even attempt a smile. "Christopher."

"I didn't mean to intrude." And he had intruded. He wasn't sure on what, but Ashley's thoughts looked heavy enough to crush her.

"No, you're just the person I was hoping to talk to." She sucked in a deep, long breath. The agonized look remained in her eyes. "You want to take a walk? The fresh air is nice."

"Absolutely."

They fell in step beside each other. He gave her the space and time she needed to pull together her thoughts. Whatever she had to say, it seemed to be a burden. He braced himself for her words. Had she secretly befriended a terrorist? He just couldn't even begin to fathom what had her so tense.

She shoved her hands deep into the pockets of her blue coat. Her steps seemed slow, uncertain almost. "So there's something I've been meaning to talk to you about."

"You can tell me anything, Ashley."

She licked her lips. "It's a little complicated, Christopher. Actually, it's a lot complicated, at least when it comes to my heart."

When it comes to her heart? Had she been mixed up with someone shady who was bad news? Fire rushed through his veins at the thought. He'd always imagined her marrying someone stable and secure, someone who'd take good care of her.

Who was he kidding? He'd always imagined her marrying him. Only that couldn't happen. War had left him warped and incapable of a committed, healthy relationship. Ashley deserved someone better, someone who wasn't consumed with the tragedies he'd faced.

She paced a few more steps, her face tight. Whatever she had to say, she was struggling.

Finally, she stopped and licked her lips again. When she looked at him, the emotion in her eyes broke his heart. "Christopher, when you left me…" She paused, her eyes wavering in thought. "When you left, I was angry."

"You had every right to be."

She heaved in a deep breath. "I didn't ever want anything to do with you again. I told myself that you'd made your choice, and that I had to get on with my life. That's what you told me you wanted."

"I did." He clearly remembered saying those words. Each one had made his heart feel like it was crumbling away, bit by bit.

"You told me that you'd chosen to be career military instead of going the family-man route, right?"

He nodded, wondering where she was going with this. "I think I did say something like that."

She squeezed her lips together and shook her head. "Look, Christopher, this is really hard for me. There's no easy way to say it."

"I'm a big boy. Don't worry about me. Just say it."

She swallowed hard. "Christopher, I— We—"

Before she could finish her sentence, an explosion sounded behind them. They glanced back to see a huge ball of fire rising up from the guardhouse at the Eyes' entrance.

# ELEVEN

"We've got to leave. We can't stay anywhere too long, or they'll find us."

Ashley nodded as she absorbed Christopher's words. She was still in shock over the car bomb that had killed the guard at the gate, as well as the driver of the vehicle who'd pulled up to the entrance with a bomb in his trunk.

They'd spent the last four hours dealing with the aftermath of the attack. Looking for survivors, calling the authorities, picking up the pieces.

Not Ashley, of course. They'd tucked her away, afraid there might be another attack. So she'd sat at the window and watched the devastation around her. Wasn't that what her life had turned into? Ground Zero after an attack?

The FBI had come in and she'd given them a statement. She'd told them about Josh and David, praying in the process that she wasn't getting them killed. Guilt had filled her when one of the agents had looked outraged over her not reporting their abduction sooner.

A rock and a hard place. She'd been there before, and it wasn't a fun place to be.

She stared out the window again, trying to find even a sprig of hope in the barrenness of her soul at the moment. "That poor guard. He looked so young."

Christopher's lips pulled into a tight line. "I know. These men are clearly trying to send a message. We've got to get you out of here. Grab your things."

She felt numb as Christopher led her back upstairs and into her room. In a trancelike state, she stuffed her few measly belongings into one of the shopping bags she'd picked up on their trip Saturday before meeting him in the hallway.

Christopher's eyes glowed with compassion as he looked down at her. She tried not to let his sensitivity to her emotions clutch at her heart. She was already feeling so vulnerable.

"You ready?"

She nodded, even though she felt anything but ready. If the terrorists could get to her inside the Eyes' headquarters, just what was waiting for her outside of these gates? She had to be strong, though, for David's sake if no one else's.

Christopher led her outside and to a waiting SUV. A moment later, they took off through an alternate exit out of the Eyes' headquarters. She remained silent as they wove through the dark streets. The sun had set at least three hours ago. In the distance, the lights from emergency vehicles still flashed, a reminder of the tragedy that had occurred.

Ashley said nothing. There was nothing to say.

Miles and miles of road passed and she stared out the window, lost in her thoughts.

Finally, they pulled down a long, winding lane surrounded by woods. A cabin, complete with the front porch light on, waited for them at the end. She sat up straighter, curiosity driving away the doldrums. "Where are we?"

Christopher put the car in park and stared at her for a moment. "It's a safe house."

"A safe house?" She blinked. She'd heard about safe houses before. She never thought she would need one, though. They were for…people in danger. That now included her. She never thought *Ashley Wilson* and *danger* would be in the same sentence.

"We'll be out of danger here tonight. We won't stay anywhere more than one night, though, just as a precaution." He opened the door and grabbed their bags from the back.

Still numb, she followed him through the darkness and toward the house. A man stood at the door, waiting for them. Christopher introduced him as a guard who'd been assigned to stay there and keep an eye on the place for them.

Ashley stepped inside. The space was small, but homey. Someone had even taken the time to light a fire and warm the air for them. It wasn't quite home sweet home, but it would do.

She couldn't let the coziness of the place allow her to let down her guard, however. She might be safe for the moment, but the moment would soon pass.

Christopher's hands went to her shoulders. She looked up at him, sucking in a breath at his closeness. Firelight danced on his face, the amber hues softening his features. For a moment—and just a moment—she felt like she was nineteen again, and young and in love. She snapped out of it and took a step back. Christopher's hands still remained on her shoulders, but she realized his touch was meant to ground her and not as a romantic advance.

"Did you want to finish having that conversation now?" he asked.

That conversation? It took her a moment to even remember what that conversation was. David. Being his son. The devastation that would follow. No, there'd been enough devastation for one day.

She shook her head. "No, not now. I just need to rest now." She was too tired. Too much had happened and she didn't want to muddy the waters any more than they already had been.

He nodded. Was that disappointment in his eyes? His hands slipped from her shoulders, and he scooted back a step. "Okay."

She turned toward one of the bedrooms down the hall, realizing just how out of control her emotions were tonight. Because for another moment there she'd felt some of her attraction to Christopher return.

Things between them would never work out. Never. Hadn't she learned that already? And when she shared her secret, their rift would become even greater. "I just need to get some shut-eye."

She fled before he could ask any more questions.

The next morning, Christopher sat at the kitchen table and stared outside. The snow still covered the ground, though it had started to melt. On the edge of the woods that surrounded the cabin, two deer found a patch of grass and nibbled there, occasionally glancing around for any signs of danger.

They reminded him, for a moment, of Ashley. She was so innocent, but she'd become like prey to the men who were hunting her. Everywhere she went, she couldn't let down her guard, not even for a second. She was graceful, beautiful...and in danger.

He sipped his coffee. He hadn't been able to sleep for most of the evening as his mind replayed what had happened over and over again. Each time he closed his eyes, that explosion rocked his world.

It sent him back to Afghanistan. Sent him back to that

final raid. Sent him back to finding Liam outside, shot down by combatants' gunfire.

He closed his eyes as the memories came again. At once, he was back on the ground beside his friend.

*"Stay with me! I'm going to get you help."*

*Liam shook his head. "No, get out of here. It's too late for me. I'll only slow you down."*

*"I'm not leaving here without you."*

*"Christopher, go! Don't let them take another life."*

*Gunfire exploded in the distance. Yells and shouts crept over the hill. The insurgents were getting closer. It was just a matter of time.*

*Before Liam could argue, he hoisted his friend over his shoulder. Then, as gunfire rained behind him, he ran toward the Humvee. He ran and ran. His lungs burned. His—*

He shook his head. He was in Virginia. So why did his mind so easily travel back to Kabul? How long would it be until the nightmares stopped?

*Lord, I know You make all things work together for our good. Even when we can't see it. I definitely can't see it now, but I pray that Your hand would be on all of this.*

A moment later, Ashley came padding down the hallway. She looked like she hadn't slept any better than he did. She pulled up a seat across from him and plopped down. "Morning."

He stood. "Coffee?"

"Please."

He brought her a cup. She took a slow, long sip and closed her eyes. "Thank you."

"How'd you sleep?"

She frowned. "I didn't. Everything just kept replaying in my head."

"Yeah, I know what that's like."

She took another sip. "Please tell me that you don't expect me to stay here with only my thoughts for company? I will lose my mind if I'm expected to sit around and twiddle my thumbs."

"I didn't take you hostage, Ashley. Even though I would prefer it if you did just hunker down. I'd feel better." Keeping her under lock and key was tempting, just for safety's sake.

She shook her head. "I've got to find Josh and David. I've got to track every lead. I've got to do something."

He nodded. Her answer hadn't surprised him, not in the least. "I know."

"I was hoping we might visit TechShare and see if Josh's boss is in."

"We can do that."

"And I never did check my voice mail yesterday. I just want to make sure there are no messages...you know, from my brother or something. Would you mind?"

He grabbed his phone from the counter. "The line is secure. Go ahead."

She began tapping in some numbers. A moment later, her lips twisted in confusion. Finally, she put the phone down and stared at him.

"This message is from one of the companies that hired me."

"What's going on?" He set his mug down.

"It's strange. He said information from his website has been compromised."

"Don't hackers do stuff like that all the time?"

She shook her head. "No, it's strange because I have multiple layers of security set up on my sites. They've never been compromised. He sounds livid. He wants to meet with me about it—with his lawyers."

"That doesn't sound good." He leaned closer. "You

should consider that this could be a setup, Ashley. This could be a way that someone's trying to lure you out of hiding. They knew putting your professional reputation on the line would draw you out."

She squinted. "You think?"

"Maybe. You never know."

"The man who called wasn't my original contact. His name is Damian Maro. He said the previous communications director left the company."

"How about if I call Denton and let him run his name through the system?"

"Might not be a bad idea."

Christopher came back into the room a few minutes later with a piece of paper in his hands. "Denton did a quick scan of his name. He said he can't find a connection with the company he claims to be with. Of course, if he's new, it could take a while to show up."

Ashley shrugged. "Maybe."

Christopher held up the paper. "Denton did find an address for a Damian Maro. Why don't we go pay him a visit?"

"Now?"

He nodded. "Yeah, when he's not expecting us."

"Let's do it."

Ashley's fingers dug into the seat as they headed down the road. What would today hold? Hopefully, she'd get some answers. She couldn't hope for all of the answers, but at least one would do. For now.

Christopher glanced over at her, his grip tight on the steering wheel. "We're near TechShare. Do you want to swing by there before going to visit this Damian guy who left that message?"

Ashley nodded. "That sounds like a plan. Maybe Josh's boss will be willing to talk to us."

Christopher pulled off the road, and a few minutes later they drove into the same parking lot where they'd stopped this past weekend. The difference was that now it was daylight and cars filled each of the spaces there. Hopefully, Josh's boss would be in and might have some answers.

Christopher put the car in park and turned toward her. "Let's go see what they have to say."

She nodded and climbed out of the car. They walked to the nondescript gray building. TechShare. She'd never heard of the company before her brother started working for them, but apparently they were responsible for a lot of the computer programs and parts that were used today.

A plain reception area greeted them as they stepped inside out of the cold. A young brunette sat behind a desk with a professional smile on her face. "How can I help you today?"

"We're here to see Garland Evans," Christopher said. He strode up to the desk, looking every bit as self-assured and in charge as he ever had. At one time, Ashley had loved that about him. If she let herself, she could easily love it again.

The receptionist's smile slipped some. "Mr. Evans? Do you have an appointment?"

Christopher shook his head. "No, but it's important that we speak with him."

The brunette quirked an eyebrow. "And you are?"

Ashley stepped forward. "Josh Wilson's sister."

Her eyes widened but only for a split second. "Let me see if Mr. Evans is available. He's a very busy man." She punched some numbers into her phone and whispered a few things into the device before hanging up and turning to them. "I just talked to his secretary. He's in meetings all day, unfortunately, but we can set up an appointment for you."

Ashley shook her head. If Mr. Evans was in this building, she had to talk to him before she left. "We drove up here just to see him. It's extremely important. It's about my brother."

"I understand, but—"

"We're not leaving until we speak with him," Christopher said. His voice sounded authoritative and sent shivers down Ashley's spine.

The receptionist's eyes widened. "One more minute."

This time, she slipped out a door leading to some offices in the back. The minutes ticked by. Finally, she came out. A distinguished-looking, gray-haired man followed behind her. He extended his hand to Ashley. "I'm Garland."

"I'm Ashley Wilson, and this is my friend Christopher Jordan."

He nodded curtly. His blue eyes looked perceptive but tired. "What can I do for you?"

"Is there a place we could talk in private?" Ashley asked.

"Of course. Let's go in the meeting room we have right here." He led them to a room off the reception area. They sat down at a gray table. Mr. Evans remained the picture of a professional with his crisp sleeves perched atop the table.

Ashley decided not to waste any more time. She locked gazes with Mr. Evans. "I'll just get down to business. I'm worried about my brother, and I wondered if there was anyone you know of who was trying to steal information on the plans he was working on for the company?"

His gaze traveled perceptively from Ashley to Christopher and then back. "Steal the information on the plans?"

Ashley shook her head, unwilling to back down—not

when the lives of people she loved were on the line. "I don't know exactly what my brother was working on. But I do know how competitive the technology field can be. Whatever project he was handling, was there any chance someone else wanted it?"

He remained silent for a moment before nodding slowly. "I suppose there's always that chance. We haven't received any direct threats, however, if that's what you're asking. May I ask why you're questioning me about this? Is your brother in some sort of trouble? I thought he was on vacation."

Ashley licked her lips. How did she answer that without giving away too much about her brother?

Christopher spoke up. "We believe someone is threatening him. We're just trying to get to the bottom of things while he's away, using his vacation time."

Garland nodded slowly, thoughtfully. "I see. I'm sorry to hear there's been a threat, but I don't believe it has anything to do with his work here. Yes, he's developing some cutting-edge technology, but I don't think it would put his life at risk."

Ashley wasn't ready to give up yet. "Is there anything else you can tell us about his work here? Anything that might give us an idea of what's going on?"

"I wish I could tell you something, but I can't. There's nothing to tell. He seems to get along with everyone here and be well respected. I wish I could help you. I really do."

Christopher cleared his throat. "So there's nothing going on here at work that you think would be the cause for any conflict?"

"As I've already said, no, there's nothing here that's cause for alarm—just a bunch of computer techies doing their job and helping technology to run a little more smoothly."

Ashley nodded, her gut roiling with disappointment. She'd hoped for so much more from their visit. "Thanks for your help."

He stood and straightened his sleeves before handing her a card. "If you need anything, let me know."

As Ashley stepped outside, all she could think was that they'd just hit another dead end.

# TWELVE

Their next stop was at Damian's house. As they sat across the street from his home, Christopher was grateful that the SUV's windows had a slight tint to them, which made it harder for anyone to see they were there. A car sat in the driveway, making it appear someone was inside the two-story, stucco-sided house.

He glanced in his rearview mirror again. Why couldn't he shake the feeling that he was being followed? He'd felt like that ever since Ashley had shown up on his doorstep. As he scanned the area around him, he saw nothing out of place. Still, he didn't let down his guard.

Beside him, Ashley hung up the phone and shook her head. "You'll never believe this. My brother called David's school on Friday and told them he was going to be out sick for a while. Why would he do that?"

Did Josh have something to do with all of this? The evidence was beginning to point to a "yes." Christopher knew it was a possibility that Ashley didn't want to consider. He settled on saying, "That surprises me."

"I also called one of Josh's neighbors about picking up his mail. While I was on the phone, the post officer came by and said that the mail had been stopped at my brother's house for two weeks. That doesn't even make any sense."

Christopher tried to find some words of comfort. "Maybe his captors made him do those things so the police wouldn't be alerted."

She shook her head. "I just don't even know what to think."

"The answers will come to light. Just give it time."

She shook her head again. "I don't have time. That's the problem. With each second, I feel like Josh and David are slipping further and further away."

He stared at the house, trying to steer the conversation away from the obscure and onto the tangible. "Tell me more about this company whose website was hacked."

"The company is local, but this website was for an online store that would complement their physical locations. I helped them set up all of their sales pages, as well as a check-out system with security verifications."

"What kind of store?"

"They sell holistic products—you know, vitamins, supplements, all natural stuff. They're a growing company. If I remember correctly, they have thirty stores, mostly here in Virginia but they're about to expand to other states."

"You said something about layers of security?"

She nodded. "It's my brother's theory. He said you need multiple layers from multiple sources in order to keep your sites safe. He helped me with that aspect of each site. That's why I have such a hard time believing that anything could have been compromised. It doesn't make any sense. My sites have never been hacked. Even Koury Pharmaceuticals hired me."

He recognized the name. "That is impressive."

"They hired me based on my record. A pharmaceutical company can't risk being hacked. People's lives are on the line if they are because the hacker could change vital information about their products. That's why this is so unbelievable to me."

He sat up and nodded toward the door. "Look, someone's leaving now. Do you recognize him?" A man, probably in his late forties with a stout build, walked toward the sedan in the driveway. His gaze shifted around him, but he kept going.

Ashley shook her head. "No, I've never met him. Like I said, his name isn't even familiar. He definitely wasn't my contact at the company."

There was a good chance that this man wasn't even with the company. As the man got into his car and started down road, Christopher eased out behind him. They followed a comfortable distance behind. Finally, he pulled in front of a restaurant in downtown Norfolk.

Good. Somewhere public. That would be the perfect place to talk to the man and find out what was really going on.

Christopher found a parking spot along the street. Once the man disappeared inside, they climbed from their vehicle, crossed the road and stepped into the neo-Southern restaurant. As Ashley started forward, Christopher pulled her back into the waiting area. The hostess stared at them suspiciously from behind her stand while patrons cast curious glances their way.

He leaned in close enough to Ashley that her hair tickled his cheek. "Easy," he muttered.

He peered around the corner and spotted the man— Damian—being seated at a corner table with two other men.

"What are you doing?" Ashley whispered.

Christopher leaned in close again, this time getting a whiff of her flowery scent. Something about the smell brought him a good measure of comfort. He nodded toward the distance. "You recognize any of them?"

She shook her head, pulling her coat closer. "Not a single one."

"If there's any place to talk to them, this would be it. It's nice and public." He glanced around the crowded space, one that was decorated with oversize roosters and sprouts of cotton stalks in milk jugs.

Ashley's eyes remained on the men. "If those are the same men who tried to shoot us in a mall, I doubt they'll blink an eye at pulling their guns here."

"They're not expecting us here. That's the difference." Still, he was well aware of the gun at his waist. He hoped more than anything that he didn't have to use it.

Ashley finally glanced up at him, a new determination in her gaze. "You should let me do the talking, just in case there is any validity in what he's saying and he actually does work for the company who hired me."

He raised his hands. "I'm just here for moral support. And protection." Of all the people he'd saved in his life, he could think of no one he desired to watch over more than Ashley. That realization caused Christopher to feel slightly off balance.

She nodded, seriousness staining her gaze. "I appreciate it."

She started toward their table, and he trailed behind. From the way she held her shoulders, he could hardly tell she was nervous. "Mr. Maro?"

The man looked up, his cool gaze accessing her. He had more bald spots than hair and wore a suit that looked expensive. Two men sat on either side of him. Both were large—both in frame and in weight—and one had an ugly scar across his forehead. What looked like tea, presumably sweet, waited in condensation-covered pickling jars in front of them, and fried green tomatoes sat in the center of the table.

Damian's eyebrows flickered up. "Yes?"

"I got a message from you about your company's website."

He squinted. "And you are?"

"Ashley Wilson."

His eyes lit and he shifted in his seat. "Ms. Wilson. How unexpected. How did you know to find me here?"

She raised her chin. "I just had to make a few phone calls."

His gaze moved back toward Christopher. "You brought police protection, I see? Off duty, I assume? Was that necessary? Perhaps it's protocol. That's what I'll believe. Better that than to be insulted." His eyes flickered. "Have a seat."

She shook her head. "I'd rather not. I can't really stay and talk very long. I'm in town so I thought I should try to meet with you during this very short window of time."

His eyes seemed to darken. "I see."

"As you can imagine, I'm anxious to resolve any issues you might be having with the site. I was concerned because in all of the conference calls with your company, your name never came up. I was surprised you were the one who contacted me."

Christopher glanced behind him. Was someone lingering outside the front door? The same shadow that he'd sensed following them since this all began? His muscles tightened as he felt danger closing in.

Damian chuckled. "As I said in my voice mail, I'm new with the company and I've been assigned to oversee this massive glitch that has us all on edge, especially since you promised a better product than what's been delivered."

Her hands went to her hips and a new fire lit her voice.

"My websites have firewalls that hackers can't get past. So why did you really want to see me?"

"I can understand why you're leery." He glanced at the two men on either side of him. "I'm also a little on edge, especially since you've confronted me here at a restaurant of all places. Why don't we talk about this back at my office?"

She shook her head. "Have you talked to Joey Anderson about any of this?"

"Mr. Anderson is the one who approached me."

Ashley's lips curled in a small smile. "Was he? That's funny, because Joey is a woman."

The man smirked. "You're a smart one. I'll hand that to you. There are many things a computer expert can do for you. Clarifying whether someone with a unisex name is a male or female is apparently not one of them."

"My brother is not involved with this." She took a step closer, looking ready to jab him in the chest to drive home her point. Christopher's hand encircled her arm and held her back.

"How about you, Ashley? Are you involved?" The man's voice remained ice cold, absent of any emotion.

"Where's my brother?"

He shrugged. "I don't know what you're talking about."

"If you hurt that little boy, so help me…" She lunged toward him again, but Christopher held her back.

Damian only smiled with that blank look in his eyes.

Christopher tugged at her, the feeling of danger closing in becoming tighter and more urgent. "Come on, Ashley. Let's get out of here."

"Going so soon? I thought the fun was just beginning."

She pulled away, back toward Damian, and sneered. "What fun would that be that you're talking about?"

"The fun where you die."

Warning alarms were sounding in Christopher's head. They had to get out of here. Now.

"Come on, Ashley. We've got to go." He pulled her toward the door.

"Tell me where David is!"

Damian smiled, that same self-satisfied smirk that made Christopher want to lunge at him also. "You'll have to find him yourself. Unless we kill you first."

The two men seated on either side of him stood. Too late. Christopher's muscles tightened. This didn't look good. Not good at all. He pulled Ashley closer.

"Why don't you two go for a little ride with my friends here? I call them Bruno and Babyface," Damian said. "They'll take good care of you."

"We're not going anywhere with you," Christopher muttered.

"Fine. We can do the dirty work here, if we must. But you'll be making more work for us, cleaning up. I suppose it will be worth it."

Christopher was all-too aware of his gun tucked into his waistband. He just had to get a hold of it somehow without drawing attention to himself. Still, even with his gun, could he take down these guys? He wasn't sure.

Another man appeared at the front door, blocking their exit.

Not this again.

Not another game of chase.

But apparently, that was exactly what they were playing right now.

He mentally counted to three and then took off toward an emergency exit door to the side. He pulled Ashley with him. Alarms wailed as soon as he opened the door, but he kept charging forward. The men trailed not too far behind.

They burst into the chilly air and darted toward their SUV. Shots fired behind them, coming dangerously close.

He hit a button on his key chain and the lights flashed on the vehicle, unlocking the doors. With the men still at their heels, they dove inside the car. Keeping his head low, Christopher jammed the keys in the ignition, cranked it, and threw the car into Drive.

"Stay down!" he yelled.

Ashley crouched on the floor. Glass showered around her as a bullet hit the windshield. Christopher squealed into traffic, narrowly missing an oncoming car.

A bullet hit their wheel. The car lurched. Ashley screamed.

He gripped the steering wheel, desperate to maintain control of the vehicle. The wheel pulled to the right, thumping along the road on the deflated tire.

He glanced in his rearview mirror and saw the men standing on the street corner, staring after the vehicle.

They were going to get away. Barely, but Christopher would take whatever victories he could.

As Ashley pulled herself back up into the seat, she glanced down at her biceps and saw the blood there. She'd been hit. In her haste to stay alive, she hadn't even noticed the injury.

But even in her haste to stay alive she couldn't outrun her memories. Her heart still pounded erratically from the drive. She instantly remembered the sound of crushing metal, the feeling of broken limbs, the panic over feeling herself begin to die.

It had been a long time since those memories had consumed her. But feeling so close to being in another accident had triggered the thoughts and sent her toppling back in time. She gripped the armrest and took a few deep breaths.

She was going to get through this. She had to. Moving forward was the only option.

From the driver's seat, Christopher touched her arm, his eyes wrinkling as he stared at her wound. "You're hurt."

She touched the cut, squinting with sudden discomfort. "I'll be okay." And she would be. Things could have turned out far, far worse.

"A bullet must have grazed you. We need to get you help." His grip on the steering wheel tightened as he frowned.

She shook her head, unwilling to stop—yet. They needed to get farther away. Those men could still find them. "It's not that bad. A bandage and some ointment will do the trick."

The SUV continued to bump down the road. They'd made it out of Norfolk and now headed north on the interstate. Ashley knew enough to realize they wouldn't make it much farther on this tire. She wasn't sure how much longer her nerves would let her continue to travel. Each bump of the tires seemed to nudge her thoughts back into the past.

Ashley stared out the window and took a deep breath. She had to focus on the present. What had that meeting been about? Just who was that man? And why were these men so brazen, so determined to get to Ashley at any cost?

Christopher pulled off the interstate. "This is the end of the road for us right now, Ashley. I'll call Denton and he'll send someone out here to help us. This SUV just isn't going to make it anymore."

A small community came into view in front of them. A river graced one side of the town and a strip of shops nestled into a cliff on the other. It looked familiar, like she'd been here before, but she couldn't place it. "Where are we?"

"Historic Yorktown."

"Nice." She pointed to a restaurant in the distance, The Revolutionary Grill. "It looks like it's open. Can we grab a bite to eat and I'll get cleaned up?" Ever since she'd smelled those fried green tomatoes, her stomach had been rumbling.

"Absolutely."

Relief filled her when they pulled into a parking space. Finally. The car ride had nearly done her in. It brought back too many memories of the accident that had nearly claimed her life.

Christopher gripped her elbow and helped her from the car and into the grill. They stepped inside the restaurant, pleasantly surprised by the warm decor. Patrons scattered the dining area, chatting quietly to each other. The place had an old-world charm about it.

A petite woman with long, brown hair greeted them at the door, a baby on her hip and an apologetic smile on her lips. "We're short-staffed tonight so I'm working with one less arm. We usually try to be a little more professional than this. Table for two?"

"Don't apologize. He's adorable." Ashley smiled. "And, yes, please. A table for two."

The woman stepped closer and pointed to Ashley's arm. "That's a nasty cut. Do you want me to get my first-aid kit for you?"

"Would you?" A bandage sounded really nice. The cut throbbed, though she didn't want to admit it.

"Absolutely." She extended her hand. "I'm Kylie, by the way. This is my and my husband, Nate's restaurant."

Ashley glanced around again, liking the place already. "It's lovely."

She grinned. "Thank you." She led them to a corner table, placed the menus in front of them, and then hurried to the back.

Ashley watched in the distance as Kylie talked to a man in the kitchen. He kissed her forehead and affectionately tousled the boy's hair before grabbing something from the cabinet. Ashley's heart lurched at the sight of the happy little family.

Having a happy little family apparently wasn't in store for her. The sooner she accepted that, the better. Seeing Christopher had stirred up those old hopes, but she had to let them go.

The man from the back approached their table. "My wife tells me you need the first-aid kit?"

Christopher nodded. "We had a little accident. If you have a bandage, that would be much appreciated."

The man put a plastic box on the table. "Here you go. Use whatever you need. If we can do anything for you, let us know, otherwise we'll leave you be." He took a step away before looking back. "And welcome to The Revolutionary Grill."

Christopher came around to her side of the booth and pulled Ashley's sleeve up. The feeling of his fingers against her skin caused shivers to shimmy up her arm.

"They seem nice," he muttered. "Nothing like a small town."

"I still love small towns," Ashley said as Christopher dabbed some ointment on her wound. She tried not to flinch. She'd never been a very good patient.

"You always did."

"One day, that's where I'll move." She tried to keep her thoughts focused on anything but her wound. It stung as Christopher sprayed something on it.

"Why not now?"

"I wanted to stay close to David." *Because he's my son.* She kept those words to herself.

He glanced up at her, his green eyes making her heart do an unwilling flip. "You really love him, don't you?"

She nodded, refusing to let the tears escape from her eyes. "More than life."

"He's lucky to have you." Christopher pressed a bandage over the cut and pulled her sleeve back down. Ashley could finally breathe again when he slipped back over to his side of the booth. He could *not* have this effect on her. It just wasn't healthy.

She licked her lips, changing the subject. "That was close back there."

He nodded and his eyes clouded. "Too close. Every lead we follow hasn't brought us any answers, just more questions. There's something we're missing."

"I wish I knew what." She felt practically willing to give her life to find out. Without answers, she was no good to anyone.

Another waitress appeared. Ashley's stomach growled, so she didn't waste any time perusing the menu. She ordered salmon served over fettuccine. Christopher picked the catfish with fries.

She glanced out the window and saw fat flakes of snow had begun to fall again. The overhead music began a soft rendition of "It's Beginning to Look a Lot Like Christmas." "Two snowfalls in four days? That's gotta be a record around here."

Christopher followed her gaze out the window. "Maybe people will have their white Christmas after all."

She twirled the ice in her glass of water. "I keep forgetting that it's only a few days away." Her gaze focused on Christopher. Maybe this would be a good time to talk about him, to at least find out some answers to the haunting questions about him. "Do you miss being a SEAL, Christopher?"

His gaze darkened, but he didn't look away. "At times."

"Why do you always get that pained look in your eyes whenever you talk about being a SEAL?"

She expected him to deny it. Instead, he shrugged and pushed his water away. "There were some rough times, Ashley. My days over there were filled with purpose and adrenaline-pumping adventure. But I've seen things that you don't ever forget."

She couldn't even imagine the things that he'd experienced. "Have you tried counseling?"

"A few times. All they want to talk about is PTSD. I don't see how that helps anything."

She cleared her throat, venturing into ground she wasn't sure she wanted to cover. Some little voice inside seemed to nag at her to take the leap, anyway. "People told me I had PTSD after my car accident."

His eyes widened. "Your car accident?"

She nodded. She didn't like to talk about it, but sometimes she knew she had to. She knew her story could help other people. "Yeah, I was hit head-on by a drunk driver."

He blinked and leaned toward her. "Really? Why didn't I hear about this?"

"I told people not to tell you." It was the truth. At least she'd gotten that much out. Maybe she'd take baby steps closer and closer toward the total and complete truth of the situation.

"Why would you do that?" A touch of hurt stained his voice.

"I didn't want you coming back to check on me out of sympathy. Besides, I didn't feel like I could handle seeing you emotionally. I already had enough other things on my plate at that point." She twirled her ice around again.

He frowned. "Tell me about what happened."

She closed her eyes a moment, hating to relive any part of the tragic ordeal. Most people were blessed enough to block out those painful moments. She'd been wide awake during the accident and even afterward when the EMTs pulled her broken body from the car. Thankfully, David hadn't been with her. "I shattered my pelvic bone, broke two ribs, my collarbone, and my leg basically snapped."

He grimaced. "I had no idea."

She nodded tightly. "I have all kinds of screws holding me together now. It was rough, to say the least. Doctors put me in a medically induced coma for a while. After that, I had months of therapy. Every time I got in a car, I had panic attacks. I kept remembering the accident. I kept waiting for another one to happen."

"You seem to do well now." The way he looked at her made her feel like he didn't see anything or anyone else besides her.

She swallowed hard and looked down at her hands. "Physically, it took a lot of therapy, but for the most part I feel like my old self. Emotionally, it took a lot of talking."

"Talking?" His head tilted.

She locked gazes with him. "I found a support group. Whenever I would feel that panic rising up in me, I'd find someone to talk to. I prayed a lot. I tried to look for the good around me."

"What do you mean?"

"I found that some of the best therapy involved simply being positive. I clung to the good instead of the pain. I could have been killed. I could have ended up in a vegetative state. I had to remember to be thankful."

Their food came, and they lifted up a brief prayer before digging in.

Christopher's eyes met hers from across the table. "I'm sorry you went through that, Ashley."

She nodded and swallowed her bite of pasta. "I don't talk about it a lot. It was a rough time in my life. But I believe that good can come from the worst situations."

A smile crept across his lips. "I've been thinking that exact same thing recently. God seems to keep sending me those reminders."

"I've realized that He doesn't always let us see the entire game plan, but He gives us the next step at just the right moment. He gives us enough to keep us going and to keep us trusting Him. I think it helps to find purpose in our tragedies, to find a way to use them for good."

His smile widened. "You're absolutely right. I couldn't agree more." He pointed to her food. "Do you remember that time we tried to make that gourmet meal?"

The remembrance was bittersweet. This was the first time they'd reminisced about what used to be between them. She nodded. "It was awful. I knew when we—if we—got married, that one of us was going to have to learn to cook or we'd be getting lots of takeout."

Silence passed between them. *Tell him,* an inner voice seemed to say.

What better time than now? What better place than here in public where he was sure to keep his emotions under control. He had to know the other part about how the accident had affected her.

She opened her mouth, determined to push the words out.

But a glance out the window showed her that Denton had shown up with another vehicle for them.

She shook her head. She'd have to wait. Again.

Eventually, she wouldn't be able to put off telling him the truth.

# THIRTEEN

Ashley threw her head back into the pillow, trying to adjust to being in another new safe house. She didn't even know where this one was. She hadn't asked.

Her mind raced and sleep eluded her. There were too many thoughts demanding her attention. Thoughts about Christopher. Thoughts about Josh. Thoughts about David. With each breath, the stark reality of each situation deepened; it became darker and more confusing.

She turned over again, wishing she could escape the painful reflections, when a sound caught her ear.

She stiffened as she listened. What was that? Had someone gotten into the house?

Another yell zipped through the air, this clearly with the word, "Stop! What do you think you're doing?"

That was Christopher. He was in trouble.

She grabbed the gun on her nightstand and threw a sweatshirt on over her yoga pants and T-shirt.

The gun trembled in her hands as she got closer to the door. She couldn't just stay in the bedroom while her friend could be in danger.

"Get back! Everyone get back!"

Her spine stiffened again. What was going on? His words weren't making sense.

Her throat dry, she pulled the door open. A dark hallway greeted her. Despite Christopher's yells, the house was surprisingly absent of any movement. She took her first step, staying close to the wall. Sweat sprinkled across her forehead.

She could do this. Whatever situation she met with in the living room, she could handle it. She just had to think with a clear head and remain calm.

"Liam!"

She took another step when a shadow appeared at the end of the hallway. She raised her gun.

"Don't shoot," a voice urged. "It's me. Agent Johnson."

The guard, she realized.

She relaxed her arms, but only for a moment. "What's going on?"

He stepped closer and nodded toward the living room. "He's having a nightmare."

Some unknown emotion clutched at her heart. "A nightmare? That's what all that yelling was for?"

He nodded. "I'm trying to figure out if I should wake him."

She fully lowered her gun. "Let me."

Her heart panged with compassion. The war had played games with Christopher's mind, hadn't it? These were more than nightmares. These were night terrors. He hadn't come back from the war unscathed after all.

She crept into the living room. The lights were off, but her eyes had adjusted to the darkness enough that she could make out the furniture. She walked to the couch and knelt there.

She watched Christopher for a moment. His muscles twitched like he was fighting some kind of invisible battle. His breathing was heavier than normal. The blanket had been kicked off.

She knew she needed to be careful. When she woke him, she had no idea what kind of mental state he might be in.

Gently, she put a hand on his shoulder. His arm was hard and solid beneath her. She gave a little shake. "Christopher. You need to wake up."

"No! It's going to blow!"

She closed her eyes, but only for a moment. "Christopher, you're having a nightmare."

"Get down!" His entire body jerked under the weight of his dreams.

She shook harder. "Christopher, wake up."

Suddenly, he sat up on the couch. He grabbed a gun—where had that been?—and pointed it directly at her. "I said get down!"

His eyes were wide, his breathing heavy.

Ashley stared at the gun, how it was aimed directly at her face. Her throat went dry and time turned into gel. "It's Ashley, Christopher. You're having a bad dream. You need to wake up."

"I said get down!"

"Christopher, it's me! Snap out of it." Cold fear sprinkled over her forehead.

At once, the trancelike state cleared from his eyes. He put his gun down and lowered his head into his hands and let out a moan. "What are you doing?" he mumbled.

She wasn't sure who he was talking to—himself or her. She put her hand on his knee and stared at him. "You were having a terrible dream."

He rubbed his face. "Yeah, I was."

She sat beside him on the couch. "Do you want to talk about it?"

He shook his head. "I never want to talk about it."

"Maybe I should have said, do you *need* to talk about it?"

He was quiet, and she let him have his moment. She rested her hand on his back. She could feel his racing heart pulsating throughout his body.

He rubbed his face again. "Every time I close my eyes, I go back to Afghanistan."

"You go back to the war." Grief clutched her heart. Life could be so hard sometimes; certain moments were so difficult to get through. The even harder part sometimes was when you didn't know what to do to help.

He rested his face in his hands, the burden he was carrying evident in his every movement. "I wait for another explosion. I wait to find another body or to hear another cry of despair from someone who's lost a loved one."

"That wears on you after a while, Christopher."

"I can't get the images out of my head. I can still hear it, smell it, feel it."

"You know you're back here now. You're safe." She wanted more than anything to be able to comfort him, to help take away some of his pain.

He nodded before leaning back on the couch, still staring straight ahead. "On a conscious level, I do. On a subconscious level…that's a different story."

"I'm sure being here in this situation with me hasn't helped anything." As she said the words, her heart sank with realization. She'd burdened him with too much by asking for his help.

He reached over and cupped her cheek. Some of the heaviness left his gaze, replaced with a tantalizing swirl of emotion that threatened to lure her in. "I want to be there for you. I've always wanted to be there for you, Ashley."

Her throat tightened. Christopher had no idea what he was saying. He was still groggy from sleep and nightmares. And it didn't matter, anyway. His actions had spoken louder than his words. Now wasn't the time Ashley wanted to talk about it, though. Now she just wanted to help him get through this moment.

Her hand covered Christopher's. Despite her logic, she fought the emotions that wanted to rise to the surface. What would it be like to give him another chance—to give them another chance?

No, she couldn't do it. Her heart wasn't ready for it.

She pulled his hand down but didn't release her grip on it. "You should rest, Christopher." She pulled the pillow onto her lap. "I'll stay with you."

Surprisingly, he didn't argue. He settled back down into the couch. She ran her hands through his hair, trying in some way to comfort him.

After a while, his breathing evened out, and he went back to sleep.


Christopher awoke feeling better rested than he had in weeks—maybe even months or years. He sat up, trying to gather his surroundings. Had he really been sleeping that hard?

Finally, the room came into focus. The safe house.

Last night flashed into his memory. The nightmare. Ashley being there. Mumbling things he wouldn't have said in his normally guarded state.

All of that confirmed to him that he was in no place to pursue a relationship—with anyone. He'd pulled a gun on her, for goodness' sake. His mind was messed up. Would it ever recover?

He glanced over. Ashley was cuddled against the side of the couch, sleeping soundly. Her hand rested on his shoulder, and his pillow was in her lap.

That's why he'd slept so well last night—because it had

been so comforting having someone else there for him. He'd been so alone for so long. Having someone else actually watch out for him for a change was a nice feeling.

But he couldn't get used to it.

He'd really appreciated the way she'd opened up to him last night about her accident. He felt like they'd taken a major step forward in their relationship. Even when he'd brought up their past, she hadn't gotten all teary eyed, but she'd actually smiled.

God made all things work together for our good. He was working in this situation, too, wasn't He? Maybe He'd never restore their relationship to what it was, but maybe they could actually be friends again. Maybe God had brought them together, each to help the other heal.

Was the accident the big secret that she'd kept from him? He didn't know. The news had come as a shock. He wished he'd been able to be there for her. He couldn't even imagine how tough those months of recovery must have been....

Ashley's eyes fluttered open and a sleepy smile crossed her face as she pushed herself upright. "Is it morning?"

He nodded. "Yeah, it sure is."

The haze cleared from her eyes, and she squeezed his shoulder. "How are you feeling?"

"Good. Terrible. I'm not sure." He sat up straighter and raked his hands through his hair. "Sorry you had to see that."

"Don't apologize." Her focus remained on him. "You have nightmares like that a lot, don't you?"

He nodded. "I wish I could say no, but I do have terrible dreams. Even if I'm not in Afghanistan physically, I just can't seem to leave mentally."

"That's a big burden to carry."

"I can handle it."

"Someone else could help you carry that burden, you know. It might not seem quite as heavy."

He glanced at her. "You mean a shrink? No, thanks."

"Talking to someone isn't a sign of weakness."

"I know you're trying to help, Ashley, but I'm fine." He stood and ran his hands through his hair again.

"Well, I just wanted to let you know that I'm there for you, if you need me. Like I told you last night, talking to other people about what I was feeling really helped me to heal. That, and a lot of prayer."

His heart lurched. Talking to Ashley sounded like a really good idea, at the moment, at least. But did he really want to go there? To open himself up like that? Some of the wounds he had were deep; some of the memories seemed permanently painful.

"Thanks," he muttered, his throat burning. He stood. When it came to fight or flight, he almost always chose fight. But when it came to his heart, flight seemed to be his go-to choice. "I need to call Denton and see if he's heard anything."

There he went, putting off what he needed to do again. Delaying getting any help. Embracing denial that he truly needed a listening ear.

Wasn't that what a SEAL was about? Being tough? Self-reliant? All this talky-talky stuff seemed so wimpy. Yet, at the same time, the idea was tempting.

The little bit that he'd already revealed to Ashley made his burden seem lighter.

He shook his head and started down the hall to call Denton. His conversation with him caused him to put his earlier thoughts aside.

They had a lead on Josh and David's location.

Ashley stared at the warehouse from the window of the SUV. Wet drops of snow fell from the sky and slid down the window, only slightly obscuring her view of the law-enforcement vehicles parked haphazardly around the building.

"You ready for this?" Christopher asked beside her.

He'd called Denton, who'd told them the FBI had caught a break in the case. It had led them to a warehouse where they suspected Josh and David had been held. Denton had asked if Ashley and Christopher could come down to the site and identify a couple of items.

The thought made the pit in Ashley's stomach grow deeper and hollower.

Finally, she nodded. "Let's go."

They walked through slushy snow and met Denton. He stood among police officers and other men in suits—FBI agents, Ashley assumed. Denton reintroduced them to FBI agents Franco and Smith again. They'd already met after the Eyes bombing.

"We're hoping you can confirm whether or not your brother and nephew have been here," Denton said, walking with them toward the warehouse. "You'll also need to give a statement to Agents Franco and Smith. This is beyond our scope, Ashley. Other people are getting hurt."

"Not to mention the fiasco at the mall," Agent Franco said. He raised bushy eyebrows, showing his disapproval that they hadn't come forward as being involved in the entire mess.

She nodded, resigning herself to give up control of the situation.

She nearly snorted at the thought.

Control? She had no control of the situation. If she had control of it, her brother and David wouldn't be held captive somewhere right now while people around continually died or were injured. She had to let go of this.

They led her inside. Christopher stayed by her side,

and, despite their past, she was grateful for his presence. A table had been set up in the center of the large room they entered. Various boxes and wires and other items Ashley couldn't identify were scattered about.

"Bombs," Christopher muttered. "They were building bombs here."

A cold chill shivered through her. These men were heartless. And they had Josh and David.

She paused by a computer. Had these men forced her brother to work on this computer? Her heart sank at the thought of what they might be going through.

"Over here is where I really want you to look." The FBI agent directed her down a hallway. Her feet scraped the cement floor. This place was so cold and impersonal. It was no place for a child.

The agent paused by a room and extended his hand as an invitation for her to go inside. She drew in a deep breath before stepping into the space. Her eyes assessed her surroundings. Some blankets lay rumpled in the corner. Some junk-food wrappers scattered the floor. An empty bottle of juice sat abandoned by the door.

She walked over toward the blankets and kneeled down. She pictured David lying there. Was this where he'd slept? Physical pain stabbed through her heart at the thought. What she wouldn't give to hold him, to give him a hug.

"We found this. Look familiar?" Agent Franco held up a piece of paper.

Ashley took it and studied it a moment. It was a hand-drawn picture of a woman beside a little boy. From the blond hair, she clearly recognized the woman as herself and the boy as David.

"Is that your nephew's?" Agent Franco asked.

She nodded. "Yeah, that's his." Her voice cracked as she said the words.

She ran her hand over the blanket. The soft folds gave her a little comfort.

Her hand hit something hard. She moved the material out of the way, trying to uncover what was lost in the heap. Finally, her fingers squeezed around the object, and she pulled it out.

Christopher leaned closer. "A pen? That's a bit of a letdown."

She sucked in a breath and shook her head. She knew exactly what it was. She'd given it to David. "No, this is a special pen. David went through a phase where he wanted to be a spy. This is a recording pen. If you press this button here—" she pointed to it "—you can record a message or a conversation."

She glanced at the men around her. Agent Franco gave her a nod, and she pressed the button.

Her brother's voice rang out. "Ashley, don't believe everything you hear. Don't trust everyone you meet. You're our only hope."

# FOURTEEN

Christopher squeezed Ashley's shoulder again. It seemed so impersonal, but what else could he do? She'd made it clear that she wanted him to keep his distance. Yet, at the same time, she obviously needed some comfort. "You did a good job, Ashley."

She nodded. She'd pulled her sleeves down over her hands and stood with her arms crossed, a faraway look in her eyes. He could only imagine what she might be thinking about. They stood in the middle of the warehouse, a cold, brittle space, probably even when the heat worked. Law-enforcement officials swarmed the building. Bomb-sniffing dogs pulled their handlers. Radios crackled.

They'd both just spent the last three hours being interrogated by the FBI and police. Ashley had told them what had happened, sticking only to the facts. She'd carried herself amazingly well, all things considered.

Right now, she stared off into the distance. Christopher remembered well how much she liked to have her own space when she was dealing with anything overwhelming, so he gave that to her now. Her eyes flickered, as if she was having some kind of internal conversation with herself…or perhaps rehashing everything that had already happened.

Finally, she turned to Christopher, pure determination shining in her eyes. "I want to visit Wally again."

"Your brother's friend?"

She nodded and nibbled on her bottom lip for a moment. "I have a feeling there's something he's not telling me. I need to ask him some more questions."

"What brought that on?"

Ashley shook her head slowly, thoughtfully. "I'm just retracing our steps. I think he's our best choice for finding out more information."

He glanced at his watch. "Let me check with Denton and Agent Franco and see if it's okay if we leave."

He hesitated before stepping away. Both men said it was fine if they left, and that they'd be in touch. The ride was silent as they made their way north to Wally's house. Ashley was usually such a chatterbox. She could talk to anyone, anywhere. But either she'd changed since they'd last known each other or this situation was nearly unbearable. Maybe both.

They waited outside Wally's house. Finally, at seven o'clock, a car pulled into the driveway. Wally got out. He looked around him as he walked to the door, almost as if he could feel their eyes on him.

Christopher put his hand on the door handle. "Let's go."

They broke free from the car and charged up the sidewalk toward Wally. The man turned around, his eyes wide with fear. "What do you want—?" He paused when he recognized them and lowered his hands. "Ashley. What are you doing here?"

Ashley tried to step forward, but Christopher tugged her back. He didn't know who to trust right now, which made nearly everyone a suspect.

"I need to talk to you, Wally," Ashley said.

"I thought we already talked." His voice sounded tense, high-pitched.

Ashley's eyes looked pleading and earnest as she stared at her brother's friend. "I have more questions."

He started walking toward the door, shaking his head as he went. "I don't know what else I can tell you."

She grabbed his arm, pulling him to a halt on the walkway in front of the steps leading to his porch. "Please, Wally. It's important."

He stared at her a moment before finally nodding. His gaze searched around him again, the action pulling Christopher's muscles tighter. "Okay, but I don't have long."

"What aren't you telling me about my brother? I know you're hiding something. I just don't know what. His life…" She swallowed. "His life is in danger."

"In danger?" He pushed his glasses up higher and shifted awkwardly. "What do you mean?"

She shook her head. "I can't tell you anything else. I only know he's in trouble. I'm trying to find some answers, and I'm afraid you're the only one who has them."

His gaze flickered once more before finally settled back on Ashley. "I shouldn't say anything. I promised on my life that I wouldn't."

"Please." The tone of voice rang of desperation, of being on the fringe of hopelessness.

He let out a short sigh and ran his hand through his hair. He paced back and forth in three-step increments before jerking to a stop and staring at Ashley. "Your brother was being investigated."

Ashley's eyes widened. "Investigated?"

He nodded. "The higher-ups at the company thought he could be selling industry secrets. That's all rumor, mind you."

"Selling industry secrets to whom?" Ashley demanded. "Another company?"

He shook his head. "No. To terrorists."

Her mouth gaped open. "Someone thought my brother was helping the other side? He would never do that."

Wally shrugged as if he wasn't quite that sure. "There's one other thing."

"What's that?" The words seemed to tumble from her mouth. Her hands gripped her arms, reminding him of someone holding on for dear life.

"Someone at TechShare apparently hacked into the federal government's computer system. Everyone thinks it was your brother. He was looking at jail time if they found him guilty."

Ashley shook her head. "You've got to be kidding me. My brother would never do that."

He raised his hands. "I'm just telling you what I heard."

Christopher stepped closer. "Why are you acting scared? Are you being watched?"

"I'm Josh's friend. Don't you think I look guilty, too? I've been on edge for the past couple of weeks. I've felt like someone was watching me. There. Are you happy now?"

"This is serious, Wally." Ashley's voice contained a touch of exasperation.

He raised his chin. "I'm well aware."

Christopher held his frustration at bay, knowing the importance of keeping a level head in the situation. But the pit in his stomach grew. And with each new sinking depth, he realized that his concern for Ashley was continuing to widen—widening enough for him to know that his heart was beginning to get involved far beyond a mere friendship level.

He stared at Wally a moment, watching the man with his nervous twitches. Why was he nervous? He felt sure the man was hiding something else. "Is there anything else you need to tell us?"

"That's all I know. I hope your brother is okay. I really do." He paused long enough to push up his glasses and glance over at Christopher. An unreadable emotion lingered in his eyes. "And I hope he hasn't gotten himself into trouble."

Christopher had been quiet for most of the way to whatever new safe house they were traveling to for the night. Ashley had a feeling that he was mulling over some thoughts, so she let him. But from the way he gripped the steering wheel, those thoughts were heavy and intense.

Her gut told her that she wouldn't like what Christopher had to say whenever he spoke again. She wasn't sure why she was so concerned about what he was thinking, when her own thoughts were a mess.

Her brother? Being investigated? She just couldn't believe it. Did Christopher?

They pulled up onto a new property for the evening. Same routine. Different guard. This time, the place was an actual log cabin, nestled away in the foothills of Virginia. If Ashley weren't so upset—and if she wasn't with Christopher—she actually might enjoy a stay here.

As soon as they stepped inside, Christopher began pacing the living room. She sank onto the couch, her gut twisting as tension filled the room.

Finally, he stopped pacing and turned toward her. "We need to talk."

Her throat burned. She remembered starting a conversation with those very words. They hadn't had a chance to finish it yet, though. She'd been delaying the inevitable. She nodded. "Okay."

He lowered himself beside her. Concern furrowed his

brows as he stared at her. "You've got to give this up, Ashley. We're in over our heads. If your brother is guilty, you could become an accomplice in all of this by trying to help him now. Leave it to the authorities."

She blinked, trying to comprehend his words. "I can't give up."

He grabbed her hand. "Don't you see we're dealing with some dangerous men here? This is above me and it's above you. We need the entire Special Forces to win this war, and all we've got is me and you. We're not enough. I can't protect you from a court of law, if that's what it comes down to. This could get ugly on so many levels."

"I can't give up." Her throat burned as she said the words.

He shook his head. "Why not? Why can't you leave this to the authorities?"

"I just can't." She could hardly breathe as she realized she'd have to tell him the truth. Reality became clear to her. She'd put it off again and again.

"Ashley, the deeper we get into this, the more I worry about you and your safety. We're talking about His People, about terrorism, about bombings. I can't understand why you won't leave this to the authorities and just concentrate on keeping yourself safe."

Her heart leaped into her throat. There was so much pressure building inside her chest that she thought she might pass out. Passing out would be too easy, though. She had to tell him the truth, and telling him the truth would be the hardest thing of all. "Christopher..."

He leaned closer. He cared about her, didn't he? She could see in his eyes, and that realization made her confession that much harder.

"Yes?" he mumbled.

Adrenaline charged through the air. "There's something I need to tell you." Her voice cracked every other syllable.

"Go ahead."

Shakes overcame her. She sat back on the couch and jammed her hands underneath her legs to quell the trembles. Nausea roiled in her gut.

*I can't do this.*

But she had to. This was the only thing that would make him realize the seriousness of the situation. Plus, Christopher just plain needed to know. It was the right thing. She'd been denying that for a long time, but lately the truth had been smacking her in the face with absolute clarity.

"Whatever it is, you can tell me, Ashley." Christopher's voice sounded soothing and sure.

Her gaze flickered up to his, and she licked her lips. She was going to get through this without throwing up. "Christopher, I don't know how to say this. So I'm just going to say it."

"Okay."

"I need to start by saying I'm sorry." Moisture filled her eyes.

His eyebrows twitched together. "About what?"

She licked her lips again, pulling back the tears that wanted to rise up. "Christopher, about a month after we broke up, I started feeling ill. I blamed it on the stress from the breakup." She glanced at her lap. "As you know, it was hard on me."

"I know, Ashley." Compassion and sorrow stained his voice.

"I finally went to the doctor to make sure everything was okay. I'd lost some weight. I felt nauseous all the time. I didn't want to get out of bed." She rubbed her hands on her jeans, praying for the courage to say what she had to say next. "I found out I was pregnant, Christopher." Her gaze rose up to meet his.

His eyes widened. "Pregnant? You were pregnant?" Waves of emotion flashed through his eyes. Disbelief. Surprise. Realization.

"What…what happened? Did you miscarry? You should have told me."

She shook her head. "I carried the baby to term. He was a beautiful boy."

"A boy?"

She nodded. "Yes, a boy. I named him David. He's your son, Christopher."

The war in the Middle East felt like a walk in the park compared to this bombshell.

Christopher stood and began pacing and running his hands through his hair. He couldn't have heard Ashley correctly. No, this couldn't be happening.

Ashley was suddenly at his side, her hands on his arm. Her eyes pleaded with him. "I'm sorry, Christopher."

He shook his head and kept pacing, moving out of her touch. "I don't understand."

Nothing made sense. That couldn't be possible. No, no, no.

Ashley's sweet voice broke into his thoughts. "I know it's a lot to soak in."

A lot to soak in? He had a son. A *son*.

Whom he'd never met.

Who could have changed his world. Given him another reason to get up in the morning. Given him another reason to fight for the future.

"How could you keep this from me?" Anger tinged his voice as he whirled around to face her.

To her credit, she didn't back down. "You were gone.

You were in Afghanistan. You'd made it clear you didn't want a family or any commitments back here at home that would distract you from your role as a SEAL. What was I supposed to do?"

"You were supposed to tell me and let me decide!"

Her hands went to her hips. "You did decide when you left me!"

He shook his head and began pacing again. "This is different, Ashley. A boy needs a father."

"He has a father. Josh adopted him."

"If I had known…" How things would have been different if he'd known. Majorly different. Entirely different.

"What would you have done, Christopher? Would you have gotten out of the military? Would you have changed your mind and married me, anyway? What would you have done?" Her voice rose in pitch.

He raked his hand through his hair. "Maybe. Maybe I would have."

She shook her head. "I wouldn't have let you marry me out of obligation. You didn't love me enough to try to make it work before. No way would I marry you because you felt guilty."

"Obligation?" His eyes felt like they might pop out of their sockets. "Ashley, marrying you was the only thing I wanted to do, and that was the problem. Your heart can't be in two places. I couldn't be fair to you and to the military."

"And you made your decision. You were going to be a military man. That was your first love."

"It wasn't like that, Ashley." He tried not to let defeat enter his voice, but with each word, he found his fight fading. Could he ever make her understand?

"I've tried for nine years to figure out exactly what it was like, Christopher, and if I haven't figured it out yet, I probably won't."

He drew in a deep breath. He didn't want to turn the conversation away from his son. *Their* son. "You should have told me, Ashley. It would have been the right thing."

She raised her chin. "I got in my accident when he was only two months old. Josh and his wife took care of him for me for all of those months. When I looked at them together—" she sucked in a deep breath "—I knew what I had to do. I knew I couldn't give him what he needed without a job, with my physical therapy, without a spouse. You have no idea how hard that pill was to swallow. I only wanted what was best for him."

He jammed his finger into his chest. "Me. I would have been best for him."

"You weren't here, Christopher." She shook her head and closed her eyes.

He sank back into the couch and buried his face in his hands. He'd been on the verge of confessing how much he cared about her. Then she'd dropped this bombshell. Any hope of rekindling what they'd had dissolved like yesterday's snow. "I just don't know what to say."

"I realize you're upset with me. I don't blame you. As much as I tried to justify what I did, I've realized I made the wrong choice and I regret that." Her voice cracked. "I'm going to give you some time to process everything."

With that, she stood and crept away. He heard the click of her bedroom door a few seconds later.

Women. Would he ever understand them? He doubted it.

He wouldn't even try right now.

Right now, he had to let the truth sink in. He was a father.

# FIFTEEN

Ashley pressed her forehead against the door. In all of her self-righteousness, she'd hurt Christopher. He'd hurt her, too, so she'd thought it was okay. But that's who she used to be. As soon as she became a Christian she should have called him and told him the truth. But she couldn't undo the past now.

The conversation replayed in her head and made the pounding there even worse. How had she expected it to go? Had she expected that he'd be delighted and smiling the whole time?

How would she feel in Christopher's shoes?

She didn't know. She just didn't know right now.

Her hand went to her stomach. All throughout her pregnancy with David she'd wondered what it would have been like to have a spouse by her side, someone who would delight in each kick and movement. Then she'd remembered that her fiancé had abandoned her, and eventually she resigned to the fact that she was alone.

A couple of people had suggested she terminate the pregnancy. She knew she could never do that. This was a baby inside her. Her baby.

Christopher's baby.

If circumstances had been different, they would have

had a wonderful life together as a family. It would have been filled with sweet evenings playing blocks and making cookies and exploring the backyard. But she'd never been a "what if" kind of girl. That wasn't the way life had worked out. Everyone made their choices and you had to keep moving forward.

So why did her heart twist with regret?

Something moved across the moonlight shining in her window.

Her lungs tightened.

A shadow.

A shadow had passed her window.

She pulled herself up straight and stared at the window. Was that a person passing by? Had the men found them? Or was that the guard just making his rounds?

Funny, she'd never noticed him walking the perimeter before.

She wanted to peer out the window, to confirm that everything was okay.

But then the image of someone seeing her, the picture of a gun aimed right at her, filled her mind, and she remained frozen.

No, she had to get a grip. She could have just been seeing things, but before she went to sound the warning bells, she needed to look.

Drawing in all of her courage, she crawled toward the wall. Remaining low, she paused beneath the sill.

It was nothing. Her imagination.

If that was true, why were her limbs shaking so badly?

Her throat burned as she swallowed. Slowly, carefully, she rose up. At the corner of the window, she leaned toward the glass.

*Please, just let me see woods and darkness. No men with guns. No leering figures.*

The outside came into view. Trees. Darkness.

Her gaze continued to scan the area.

The movement she'd thought she'd seen was just a bird. Nothing to be worried about. Those men hadn't found them. Again.

Her gaze reached the far side of its scope. So far, so good.

A slight movement at the side of the window caught her eye. She sucked in a scream. A man was pressed there, right against the side of the house next to her window.

And he was staring directly at her.

Christopher was still fuming mad. He couldn't sleep, which was nothing unusual. Instead, he paced the living room, hoping the movement would help to sort out his thoughts.

How could she? *How could she?* That was the question that kept replaying in his mind. He'd thought more of Ashley, never that she'd be one to pull a stunt like this. She was always so well thought out and planned. She always put other people's needs above her own. She was—

"Christopher, someone's outside."

He jerked his head toward the hallway and saw Ashley standing there with wide, panic-filled eyes. He stopped pacing, adrenaline crackling through the air. "What do you mean?"

She pointed with her thumb over her shoulder. "I mean, there's a man outside my window." Her voice cracked as her words tumbled out.

His senses instantly went on alert, and he put his emotions aside. "Just one?"

"I only saw one." Her gaze darted around the room. "Where's Bruce?"

"He should be at the front door." He paced over to the

area, but there was no one there. He took a few steps closer, his hand going to the gun at his waist. "Maybe he stepped outside for a moment." Even as he said the words, cold reality hit him. Christopher was never one to be blissfully optimistic. If Bruce wasn't inside, there was a good chance he was in trouble.

She shook her head. "I hope not."

"Stay back." He walked toward the front door, bracing himself for battle.

"You're not going out there, are you?" Ashley's voice held a hint of desperation, of fear.

He didn't want his heart to soften, but it did, anyway. He paused and lowered his voice. "We can't sit here and wait for whatever's going to happen. I've got to see what's going on."

"But if you walk outside you're an open target." Her fingers dug into his arm.

He stepped closer, keeping his voice even. "I'm trained. I'll be fine. Besides, I'm not going down until I meet my son."

Her cheeks flushed. At least she had the decency to look halfway embarrassed. He cast those thoughts aside. There would be time for them later.

Ashley swallowed, her throat muscles looking tight and rigid as her hand slipped away from his arm, and she stepped back. "Be careful, Christopher," she muttered, her voice barely above a whisper.

Apprehension stretched across his shoulders as he put his hand on the doorknob. On the mental count of three, he pulled the door open. An empty porch waited for him.

He listened carefully for a sign of something—someone.

Nothing. He heard nothing.

The woods beyond the house appeared empty, but the dark spaces there could easily conceal someone.

But what if Ashley had simply been seeing things? What if it was just Bruce pacing the perimeter of the house? Still, her fear had been genuine.

He had to check things out.

He took his first step outside, his senses attuned to every movement, every sound. He held his gun, his muscles rigid and ready to fight. The cold air was no match for the beads of sweat that formed across his forehead.

A son. His son. He had to stay alive to meet him.

He had to find him to meet him.

He stayed close to the wall of the house as he crept around the building. His footsteps were light, not making a sound. Stealthlike, just as he'd been trained.

He paused at the corner then peered around.

Still nothing. No one.

Then a stick cracked in the distance.

Tension ratcheted his muscles. Someone was out there.

He raised his gun. Just what were they planning? How many people were out there exactly?

*Lord, some supernatural help might be nice right about now.*

Another stick cracked until a figure appeared from the woods. The man raised his hands in surrender as he approached. "We need to talk."

Christopher still aimed his gun directly at the man's chest. Adrenaline pumped through him. Images of Afghanistan flashed back. Insurgents. Suicide bombers—

No, this wasn't Afghanistan. But these men might be just as deadly.

"Who are you?" Christopher growled.

The man's hands remained raised in the air. As he came closer, Christopher noted that the man was probably in his late twenties with dark hair and he wore all black. "It's a long story. I'd like to explain."

Christopher didn't trust *that* easily. "Where's Bruce?"

"He's okay. I just had to get him away for a few minutes so we could talk alone. With Ashley."

"I'm not letting you get anywhere near her." Christopher examined the man more closely. Why did he seem familiar? Like he'd seen his face in the crowds before? "You're the man who's been following us, aren't you?"

"I can explain. If you'll let me." The man's eyes looked honest. But the best of them could fool anyone.

Christopher kept his gun raised. "You better start explaining now before I pull this trigger."

The man shook his head. "Listen, you don't want to do that. I'm on your side."

His muscles slacked—but just for a moment. "I'm not so sure about that."

"Please, I'm with the CIA. I was assigned to track Ashley Wilson, to make sure she wasn't working for His People. Like her brother."

Ashley stared at the dark-haired man sitting across from them. Christopher had his cell to his ear and his gun aimed at the man. The CIA? Could the man's story get any bigger or more glorified? There was no way she was caught up in some real-life spy mission. No way.

Christopher lowered his phone and sat down beside her. "Denton confirmed that he's legit," Christopher muttered.

The man—Ed Carter, he'd said his name was—nodded. "We worked together for two years. Mark Denton is a good man."

Ashley wasn't in the mood for chitchat. "Tell us where Bruce is," Ashley demanded.

The man raised his hands and patted the air as if to

say "calm down." "I will, but only after you listen to me. I'm on a need-to-know basis. You're not even supposed to know who I am, let alone your guard. Trust me. He's fine."

Fire ignited in her veins. "Trust you? I don't even know you. Why would I trust you?"

He reached into the pocket of his coat and pulled out his badge. "I'm with the CIA. My name is Ed Carter. I'm twenty-nine years old, and I've been trailing you for the past four days."

"Why are you here? Why are you talking to us?" Christopher asked. "I want some answers. Now."

The man raised his hands again. "I know. I know. And I'm going to give them to you." He turned toward Ashley. "Maybe I should start with this explanation. TechShare is just a cover name for a CIA office."

She blinked, trying to comprehend what he was saying. "A CIA office? What are you talking about?" There her mind went again, feeling like she was in the middle of some spy movie. Only this wasn't a movie. This was her life—her upside-down, crazy, how-had-she-gotten-here life.

Ed Carter didn't blink as his gaze connected with hers. "Ashley, your brother didn't work for a corporation that was developing new computer software. He was recruited by the CIA to work in our cyberterrorism division. Your brother was not only proficient in hacking into systems, but he was also quite talented at developing viruses. He was, quite frankly, a genius."

Where was he going with this? "So he was abducted by His People for his knowledge?"

Ed's face remained grim as he shook his head. "Not quite. We think he was working for His People all along. We think he's giving them information, for a price."

She stood. "For a price? What are you talking about? My brother would never do that!"

Christopher pulled her back down. "Just hear him out, Ashley."

Fury warmed her blood, though. How could this man think that? What proof did he have?

"Ashley, we found a large deposit that had been made into your brother's checking account. We traced the money back to His People. There have been other signs that he's been doing some illegal things. We think he started playing hardball with them and that's when they snatched him."

She shook her head. "I don't believe you."

"I'm telling the truth, Ashley."

"Don't you guys always lie? Isn't that what you do? Twist things around to get what you want?"

He stared at her, not bothering to repeat what he'd already said. Which made her even madder.

She heaved in a deep breath, trying to maintain her control. "Why have you been following me?"

Ed leaned on his elbows, looking casual and as if he did this sort of thing every day. "We suspected your brother may have been working with someone. We thought it could be you. I was hoping you would lead us to your brother."

"You were the person who was outside his house that evening while Christopher and I were searching through his things," Ashley said.

He nodded. "I was. I was there when the men demolished your house, Christopher. I've pretty much been your shadow since we realized Josh had disappeared."

Ashley shook her head, trying to comprehend everything he was saying. "Why didn't you just follow those men in order to find my brother? Wouldn't that make more sense?"

"They're all just henchmen. They won't lead us to the person we need to find."

Christopher shook his head. "What do you mean?"

"I mean, if we cut off their funding, then we essentially cut them off. But no one knows who's giving these people all of their money. He's guarded like a treasure. But someone, somewhere has got to be able to lead us to him."

"You thought I was that person?" Ashley pointed to herself.

"It was our best guess. I've realized you're looking for him yourself. That's become obvious. It's also become obvious that with the two of you being together, they can kill two birds with one stone."

"What are you getting at?" Christopher asked.

Ed stared at Christopher. "I think you know what I'm getting at. Someone took down Abar Numair, the man who started His People. They may have restructured since then, but they don't easily forget. Having you involved in this case is like a bonus to them. If they can kill Ashley and one of the SEALs who helped bring their leader down, then they're twice as happy."

Christopher straightened beside her. "No one knows I was on that team."

"No, but if they had a computer hacker working for them, they might be able to find out highly classified information like that." He raised an eyebrow as his words settled over them.

A chill spread through Ashley. This was getting worse by the minute. Maybe she didn't want to know the truth. Maybe she should just find David and Josh, and not worry about any of the details.

But she knew she couldn't do that.

"Let's say all of that is true. How about me? I don't understand why they're trying to kill me. Why don't they just let me fade into obscurity?"

"My theory, once I realized you weren't working for them, is this. You saw your brother being abducted, and they wanted to make a statement that no one could get in their way. You could identify them and possibly even offer clues that would lead authorities to them—at least lead them closer. They don't want anything or anyone to get in the way with their plan."

She shook her head. "This is all crazy."

"I know."

Christopher shifted beside her. "Why come out tonight and let us know who you are?"

"It was time. I realized you weren't working for the other side. I'm going to be in and out, but I'll help you when I can."

"Is there something you know that you want to tell us?" Ashley asked.

"Your brother and nephew are on the move. They don't stay anywhere for very long. Those men want you, for some reason. You need to be careful. Very careful."

Ashley nodded, her shivers intensifying.

Death was chasing her.

The question was: Would it ever catch her?

# SIXTEEN

After Ed left, Christopher found Bruce tied up in the shed. Apparently, he'd been knocked unconscious but unharmed. Christopher had welcomed the chance to be away from Ashley and the whirlwind of emotions she always brought with her, even for just a moment.

How could she?

He couldn't stop asking himself that question. But at the same time, he had to focus on the bigger picture right now. How was he going to find his son and keep him safe?

He walked back into the cabin and spotted Ashley sitting on the couch, her knees pulled to her chest, and a far-off look in her eyes.

He didn't want to feel sorry for her. He really didn't.

But his heart couldn't help but pang with compassion.

"If I had my way, I wouldn't be around you right now," he started. "It's going to take me some time to process everything that's happened."

She blanched. "I deserve that."

"But we don't have any choice but to work together. Not if we want what's best for David. My son."

"Our son." Her features looked strained as she said the words. Suddenly, she sat up straighter, a new light in her eyes. "Maybe we can switch roles with these men. Maybe we can chase them for a change."

Her words caused him to freeze. "How? And what would that prove?"

She shrugged. "Lure them out and then follow them. Maybe they'd lead us to David. Maybe they'd at least lead us to someone who could tell us where David is."

He shook his head, thinking that sounded like the worst idea ever. "I don't know if we'd be able to lure them out, Ash. As soon as they spotted us, they would just shoot."

"Not if they didn't know it was us. Not if we were hard to recognize. I know we still wouldn't have much time. But it's better than nothing, isn't it?"

He shook his head. It was true. It was something. But so many things could go wrong. "I don't know…"

"Think about it, at least." She stood. "In the meantime, can I use the computer? I want to think through a few ideas."

"The less you're on the computer, the better. Whoever these guys are, they seem to know their way around the web. Even with the firewalls I have, I worry that they'll somehow trace you."

"I'll be quick. Only a few minutes."

He stared at her another moment before finally nodding. "Please, be quick. Until these guys are behind bars, we need to take every precaution possible."

He grabbed the laptop from his room and handed it to Ashley. Then he kept himself busy by making some coffee. There was no more sleeping for him tonight. His adrenaline was pumping too hard.

They did need another plan of action. But what? Was Ashley's idea one worth considering? Or would it just get them killed?

He didn't know.

"What…?" Ashley gasped.

That familiar tension returned to his shoulders. He strode up behind Ashley, wondering what was wrong.

"This can't be right," she muttered.

"What?"

"Someone drained all the money from my bank account."

He peered closer. Sure enough, all the money was gone. Not only that, but someone had overdrafted by hundreds of dollars.

"With the right technology and know-how, you can do anything. Someone obviously hacked into the bank's system and stole your identity." The question was: Had her very own brother done that? Even the CIA was investigating him.

But he knew Josh, and couldn't imagine him ever doing anything that might harm his sister. Perhaps someone had put the deposit in Josh's bank account in the same way they'd taken money from Ashley's. Maybe someone had set him up.

"I've got to see if there are any messages from David again."

"Don't click on them if there are. That's the only computer I've got."

She nodded and began tapping away. She leaned toward the screen. "I don't believe it."

Did he want to know? "What now?"

"It's an email from Damian. He said there's more to come if I don't give up the information."

"What information?"

"I have no idea." She glanced up at him. "But this could be just the bait I need."

Ashley shifted nervously as the wind hit her. She leaned against the railing of the outdoor ice skating rink, trying to look casual.

Only a few feet away stood Christopher. He wore a baseball cap and an oversize coat. He stood close enough to help her, need be, but far enough away that it didn't look like they were together. All around the rink, there were undercover law-enforcement officials, each looking casual and unassuming.

The plan had been set in motion. It had taken a lot of prodding and some quick planning, but here they were. The FBI, the local police, and Eyes had all gotten involved.

This was a gamble. Ashley knew that. But she was running out of options.

So many things could go wrong. Christopher had said that much.

Even as mad as he was at her, Ashley knew that he didn't want any harm to come to her.

Her breath came out in a frosty puff in front of her as Ashley watched, from across the way, a woman approach the rink. She wore Ashley's coat, was approximately her height, and had a wig on. She also wore a bulletproof vest under all of her other layers.

Ashley's stomach twisted with anxiety. Would this actually work?

It felt like her last hope. She desperately wanted to take this game of chase into her own hands. She'd never find her son if all she did was run from the bad guys.

Her gaze scanned the area again, looking for a sign of something suspicious. A man in a black overcoat approached the opposite side of the rink. Was this man one of His People?

Christopher peered over the top of his newspaper. Ashley attempted to take another sip of her coffee, but her hands trembled so badly she feared they'd give her away.

So many things could go wrong.

But they wouldn't. She had to stay positive.

There were various agents waiting in cars around the complex. As soon as the men took off, they'd follow them. Hopefully, they'd get some answers.

She'd had to beg Christopher to even let her come at all. She knew it was a risky move being here, but she'd never been very good at being passive. Being passive would not lead her back to David.

A few more people joined the skating rink fun. Most of them went directly to the ice. Ashley noticed another man, this one wearing a black leather jacket, who sat on a bench not too far away.

Was he one of the men who'd chased them at the mall? One of the men the police were looking for? Perhaps it was Babyface or Bruno. She couldn't tell from where she stood.

Her throat burned as she swallowed. Luckily, most children were in school right now. But there were still enough innocent bystanders around that things could turn ugly.

*Please protect everyone,* she prayed silently. *And please forgive me for not telling Christopher sooner. Please help me to forgive myself.*

After seeing the look in Christopher's eyes—the utter devastation—she'd had a moment of 20/20 hindsight. She should have told him from the start.

What if he never got to meet his son?

There she went again. She had to think positive.

Two men approached the decoy.

This was the moment, Ashley realized, when they'd find out if their plan worked or not.

The men closed in around the woman in the distance. Around them, people skated, totally clueless as to what was going on. Clueless about the danger that could erupt.

Ashley's gaze focused on another man who'd joined the area. He wore a blue coat and a ball cap. He didn't look familiar.

So why did Ashley have a feeling he was a part of all of this somehow? She kept her gaze on him.

He pulled out a cell phone and began talking to someone. His gaze was on the two decoys. Was he an Eyes agent? FBI? Or His People?

The other two men moved closer and closer. With the utmost professionalism, the men from Eyes blended in, not showing a sign that they were actually soldiers and law enforcement.

Her gaze went back to the man in the blue coat. She tried to make eye contact with Christopher, but his hat was pulled down low. He was attuned to everything happening with the setup.

It worked. They'd lured the men out of hiding.

But now what? Her hands shook harder until finally she threw away her coffee, put her phone in her pocket, and shoved her hands in after it.

Something shiny gleamed from beneath one of the men in black's jacket. A gun. He was going to shoot.

"Everybody down!" someone yelled.

Nervous gasps and screams spread through the crowd. One of the men raised his gun, no longer hiding its presence. He aimed at one of the decoys and fired.

Screams from the crowd became louder as people scrambled away.

Her gaze went back to the man in the blue jacket. He remained there, unmoving. Just what was his role in all of this?

The Eyes agents drew their weapons.

The man in blue took a step away.

Ashley hurried toward Christopher. "Come on."

"What are you doing?"

"We've got to follow him!"

"Who?"

"Just trust me!"

Christopher began jogging beside her. The man in blue spotted them and took off in a sprint. Ashley's legs burned as they chased him through the streets of downtown Norfolk. He darted across an intersection. Ashley looked both ways. It would be tight, but...

Drivers leaned on their horns, letting them know their displeasure at being stopped. But Ashley and Christopher kept going.

As they ran, Christopher pulled out his phone and explained to someone what they were doing. Ashley heard him muttering something about needing a car.

The man turned the corner, out of sight for a moment. Christopher grabbed her hand. His legs were longer than hers, but he pulled her along, not letting her slow down.

She didn't want to lose any momentum, even though her lungs screamed and her muscles ached. They had to follow this man.

Sirens sounded from across town. What was going on at the skating rink? She'd have to wait to find out.

The man came into sight again. This time, he had a gun in his hand. A bullet fired past them.

"Get down!" Christopher pulled her behind a car as another spray of bullets flew past them. She huddled behind a tire, her hands covering her head. Her heart beat furiously and she could hardly take a deep enough breath to fill her lungs.

Christopher peered up.

"He's getting into a car," Christopher muttered. "He's going to get away."

Christopher's heart pounded in his chest. The man couldn't get away. He might be their only link to finding his son.

Above them, the windshield of the car shattered as another bullet pierced the air. But his gun remained in his holster. The last thing Christopher wanted was to open fire in a busy metropolitan area. There was too much risk for casualties.

Ashley gasped beside him as another bullet flew past them. People ran screaming from the area. They scattered with fear.

The entire downtown seemed to be holding its breath, waiting for whatever would happen next.

They had to chase that vehicle. Now.

Just then, a car squealed around the corner and stopped beside them. Denton peered out the driver's-side window. "Get in!"

They hopped into the backseat just as Denton peeled off down the street. The car in front of them swerved before weaving in and out of traffic. Denton stayed on their trail.

Beside him, Ashley gripped the seat with terror, each turn tossing her across the car. Quickly, Christopher reached across her and strapped her seat belt over her. He then pulled on his own. This was going to be a wild ride.

Denton was capable, but they had to take every precaution.

The car in front of them turned sharply onto a street and gunned the engine. Cars swerved out of the way to miss the oncoming vehicle.

Denton threw on brakes, turning quickly to keep up with the car. The car fishtailed before righting itself. Ashley gripped his arm with white knuckles, her eyes as big as full moons.

Certainly she had to be reliving the accident that had nearly killed her. He gripped her hand, trying to bring her back to reality. He knew what it was like to get sucked into bad memories.

Denton gained on the car. A glance at the dash showed he was traveling at ninety miles an hour to catch up. Dangerously high speeds for the middle of a metropolitan area. Dangerously high speeds for anywhere.

Christopher's eyes widened when he saw a train coming in the distance. The car in front of them kept speeding forward. He held his breath, anticipating what would happen next.

The gunman was going to try and beat the locomotive across the tracks.

He clutched the armrest.

The train barreled forward.

The car in front of them didn't slow.

Their collision appeared more and more imminent.

Denton pressed on the brakes. "No way. I can't do it."

The car in front of them reached the tracks. Just as the front wheels began to cross, the locomotive engine collided with the vehicle. Metal screeched. Glass shattered. Flames exploded.

Christopher pulled Ashley's head into his chest as a small cry escaped her. Denton's car came to a complete stop, and they all stared at the tragedy in front of them.

A tragedy on so many levels, he couldn't help but think. So many levels.

Ashley leaned against the car, watching the destruction around her. The scene seemed too familiar. The burning of melted metal and plastic. The loss of life. The hopelessness of feeling like she'd never find Josh and David.

It brought back fresh memories of her accident and the agonizing decisions she'd made afterward. Life was full of unexpected turns and twists. Some of those changes were good; some knocked you off balance; some seemed to seep into your soul.

Every time she looked at the mangled metal in front of her, she was pulled back in time to that horrible night when she'd been driving home from the store. She'd seen the oncoming car traveling down the two-lane road. She'd been headed to pick up David from her father's house. Thank goodness her baby hadn't been with her. At the last minute, the oncoming car had swerved into her lane going 45 miles an hour.

She hadn't had the blessing of unconsciousness. No, she'd felt all the tear-inducing pain. Seen every agonizing moment as passersby tried in vain to help. She'd smelled the burning metal, tasted the blood in her mouth, heard the urgency in people's voices.

Staring at the scene now, each limb trembled. Her breaths came too quickly. Each sound made her jump.

Christopher's hand clamped down on her shoulder. "Are you okay?"

She shrugged. "Trying to push away the bad memories—the old ones and the new ones."

He squeezed tighter. "I understand."

They shared a smile. If anyone understood, Christopher certainly did. "I know." Despite the strain between them, he still acted out of integrity to help her. That meant a lot to her.

Emergency-management personnel continued to clean up the scene. No one had imagined it happening like this. That man had to have known he would die when he pulled in front of that train. He'd rather die than betray his loyalties. That was dedication. Or insanity, depending on how one wanted to look at it.

"It was a good try, Ash. We almost had them," Christopher muttered.

Ashley shook her head. "Almost doesn't get me any closer to Josh or David."

"We'll get there eventually."

She dared to look at him. "What if it's too late?"

"It won't be." He pulled her toward his chest again. She didn't fight him. If he wanted to hold her up, then so be it. She needed something to help her stand. She had her faith, but even that was starting to feel fragile. She knew God didn't always answer prayers in the way she wanted, but that He still had a plan regardless. Right now, she was having a hard time trusting that plan.

She stepped back and cleared her throat, trying to focus her thoughts. She turned toward Denton. "What happened at the rink?"

Christopher's hand slipped away, and she instantly missed it. Why did her heart and her mind so constantly clash?

"The FBI took one of the men into custody, but he's not talking."

A worse thought slammed into her mind. "Was anyone hurt?" *Please, no more people hurt. There's been too many already.*

Denton shook his head. "No. Thank goodness."

Relief washed over her heart but just for a moment. They had a man in custody, she rationalized. Maybe they'd get some information from him.

But why did she have a feeling they wouldn't?

# SEVENTEEN

Four hours later, they were at another safe house in another location in another town. Christopher was in the shower, and Ashley was curled on the sofa, trying to make sense of her thoughts. Finding any logic in this mess seemed impossible.

She'd already taken a shower and towel-dried her hair before she pulled on some yoga pants and a long-sleeve T-shirt. She'd tried to let the steam evaporate the memories that flashed through her every time she closed her eyes. If only it was that easy.

Where did they even go from here? She wouldn't give up—she couldn't. She'd keep fighting until she found David and Josh, even if she had to go at it alone.

She glanced across the room. Christopher's computer was on the kitchen table. He'd warned her to stay away from it, warned her that her every keystroke could be traceable. Even with the firewalls and precautions Eyes had made, these His People cronies were good enough that nothing was safe. Still, the laptop seemed to call to her, to beckon her to investigate.

The computer, technology, the internet…that's where the answers were, she realized. And that may be the only place she was going to find any answers about her brother, any of that help that her brother had alluded to when he said she was *their only hope.*

She could still hear the water pounding in the bathroom. Christopher probably had a good five minutes before coming out. She could do a lot in five minutes, and certainly she couldn't be traced in such a short amount of time.

Quickly, she scrambled over to the table. She opened the laptop and booted up the system. A moment later, she pulled up her websites. Her brother had helped her develop the security layers for each site. Had he somehow manipulated the security variants on her site? Why would he do that?

She went to the website of her biggest client—Koury Pharmaceuticals—and pulled up the site's interface. She stared at the administration page. Was there anything different? She searched through the different levels, looking for something—anything—before shaking her head. Everything appeared to be normal.

So what was wrong? Anything? Or was she looking too hard for something that wasn't there?

Most of the site was static, and the only thing that ever changed was the "comments" section. As a last resort, she clicked on that page to see the new feedback people had left. She scanned through each statement. Nothing.

The only place she had left to look was in the spam folder. She knew there would mostly be advertisements there from other online businesses, but she clicked there, anyway. Just as she thought—it was just junk.

Except one made her freeze.

There was a comment from Charlie Brown. She used to call her brother that when they were young. Her fingers trembled as she clicked the comments. The first line read, "Home for the Holidays."

Had her brother found a way to email her? Or was this a virus? Or a trick?

She read the rest of the message. "I can't wait to see you at home for Christmas. I wonder if the old tree house is still standing?"

The old tree house?

Was he talking about the house where they'd grown up? They'd had a tree house outside where she and her brother used to play. One year, they'd even reenacted *A Charlie Brown Christmas* with their friends.

"What are you doing?" a voice boomed behind her. "Are you trying to lure blood-hungry terrorists right to our doorstep?"

She nearly jumped out of her seat. She twirled around to see Christopher standing there, water still dripping from his hair. Fire flamed in his eyes.

"I'm following a hunch. I think I found a message from my brother."

His eyes narrowed. "Are you sure?"

"Of course I can't be sure. But this one spam message mentioned things that only he would know about."

"But you're not sure, and that's the point. I asked you to stay away. Every time we get on the computer, something seems to go wrong. I thought we agreed?"

She stood, not ready to back down. "The computer is the key here! I don't know why or how or what, but somehow this all ties back into technology. I'm not going to find my brother without a computer. I'm sure of it."

He stepped closer and glared down at her. "And I'm sure that if you don't stop using that computer, then you're going to die."

"Why do you even care?"

His hands flew in the air. "Of course I care! I've always cared."

"You could have fooled me!" What was he talking about? He'd made it clear that he didn't care. How could he deny that?

"Ashley—"

"No, don't Ashley me." She shook her head and jabbed her finger into her chest. "At least I owned up to my mistake. At least I showed some regret."

His face softened. "Ashley, there hasn't been a day that's gone by that I haven't regretted breaking up with you."

His words felt like ice water in her face. She backed up as disbelief filled her. "You don't mean that."

"Of course I do. I questioned myself a million times. I missed you. For almost a decade, I've missed you."

Her throat squeezed with emotion. "You never told me any of that."

"Of course not. I didn't expect you to wait around. That wouldn't be fair. You were supposed to meet a great guy and have all the happiness you deserved."

"You were the only *happiness* I wanted."

"I'm ruined, Ashley. War has messed me up. I can't ever see myself in a healthy relationship again."

"You can't see it or you're afraid to see it?"

They stared at each other a moment, something unspoken between them. Christopher's hands reached for her arms, and he pulled her closer. Something unseen—and strong—seemed to draw them closer. For a moment, Ashley felt young and infatuated again. Christopher raised his hand and stroked her cheek.

"Ashley—"

A loud knock sounded at the door. They both jumped back from each other. Christopher ran a hand through his wet hair and strode across the room. The guard stood there. "Denton just radioed me. Said you're not answering your phone."

Christopher stomped away. "My phone's in my room. Let me call him."

She still had to tell him about Charlie Brown.

Christopher's head swam in confusion. Could Ashley still have feelings for him? Was that even possible? But for a moment—and just a moment—he thought he saw that old, familiar affection in her gaze.

Then the knock on the door had sounded. It was just as well. All of their emotions were heightened right now. The last thing either of them needed was to do something they regretted.

He escaped to his room and dialed Denton's number. "What's going on?"

"The guy the FBI took into custody today gave us an address."

His hands went to his hips, something sounding way too easy about that discovery. "Why'd he give that up?"

"Plea deal. We're headed there now."

He grabbed a piece of scrap paper and a pen from the nightstand. "Where?"

"1020 Lindsey Lane in Chesterfield."

"Got it."

He ran a towel through his hair again and then threw his clothes in the bag. He was going to watch the raid. He needed to be there and see this for himself.

He paced back into the hallway to tell Ashley that he had to step away for a while. He wanted to be there if they did find Josh and David. Ashley would want him to be there.

Ashley's eyes widened when she saw him. "Where are you going?"

"They got a lead. I want to be there and see how it pans out."

"You're not leaving me."

He shook his head. "It's not safe for you to be there."

"You better believe I'm going to be there." Her jaw set in that familiar, determined way.

But he shook his head again. "Not a good idea."

"Where are you going?"

"Chesterfield."

Her eyes widened. "1020 Lindsey Lane, by chance?"

He paused. "How'd you know?"

"Because that's the house where Josh and I lived through elementary school before we moved down to Virginia Beach. That's what I was trying to tell you."

He let her revelation sink in. Maybe the information was legit. But if it was, then why did his gut still twist like something was wrong? "I don't like this. It just seems too easy."

"I'd say the same thing if I hadn't seen that email."

"Someone could have faked it, known about the nickname."

She shook her head. "I was never allowed to call Josh that except around family. No one else knows the nickname. If someone knows it, it's because Josh told them and he wouldn't do that."

He nodded toward the door. "I've gotta go."

"Take me with you. Please."

"What if it's a trap?"

"I'll be careful. I'll stay in the car if I have to. I just want to be there."

He paused, feeling his resolve crumbling. Finally, he nodded. "But only if you promise to stay on the perimeter. No sneaking off to check computers or do any investigating on your own. We don't know if this email is legitimate or not."

She nodded. "It's a deal. I promise."

He waved for her to follow. "Let's go, then."

Ashley stood on the edge of the property, close to a line of police cars and other unmarked sedans. Apparently, the FBI had been called in. She'd also seen Ed Carter. This bust was a big deal.

She prayed her brother and David would be discovered safe and sound.

Denton swaggered over to her, a walkie-talkie of some sort in his hands. She waited for him to give an update, but he shook his head. "Nothing yet. They're still testing out the place, making sure it's safe."

She nodded, her throat dry. That's where Christopher was. In the line of duty. Ever the soldier.

"Can I tell you something?"

She glanced up at Denton. "Sure." Tension squeezed her neck muscles as she said the word.

"Christopher wore the reality of his decision to break up with you every day. He did a great job covering it up and putting on his soldier's face when he was working. But I knew him well enough to see his struggle."

She shook her head, unable to accept what he said. "I realized it was hard for him. It was hard for me, too. Maybe I should be more compassionate and understanding. But all I feel is hurt. Every woman wants to be the 'one' a man would do anything to be with. No woman wants to be second place."

He shifted his weight. The overhead streetlight cast shadows across his eyes. "Let me explain it to you like this, then. Christopher is practically legendary in the Special Ops community. He's the one who took the shot and brought down Abar Numair."

"The leader of the terrorist group? The one who was all over the news?" Her eyes widened. "He was the sniper?"

Denton nodded. "Yeah, it was Christopher. It was a hard shot to make. His life was in danger. If he'd been caught, he would have been tortured long and hard. Death would have been a welcome relief."

She shivered at the thought.

"Ashley, do you realize what the sacrifice of his personal happiness means? It means that thousands of people aren't going to die at the hands of Abar Numair. It means Americans are safer, that there's less threat of a terrorist attack. His decision may have broken your heart, but his decision has saved thousands of lives."

Reality washed over her. Christopher's decision to dedicate himself to the military really had been self-sacrificing. Ashley had always known that his service was important—even if he only saved one person. But the entire scope of what he'd done became clear.

She closed her eyes as guilt began pounding at her temples. She really had been selfish, hadn't she? She hadn't been able to see any of that before now, though. She'd only been able to see her own pain and feelings of rejection.

Guilt filled her, but was immediately replaced with... love? Could that be what that emotion was? Love and pride and the biggest desire she'd ever had to reconcile with someone?

She had to talk to Christopher. She had to tell him finally that she understood. That she was wrong. She had to ask for a new start. For forgiveness.

Her gaze latched on to the house in the distance. That's where he was now.

She turned back to Denton. "Thank you, Denton. I

needed to hear that. I needed to hear it eight years ago, I suppose."

"Everything happens in God's timing. Right now is the time for understanding."

She nodded and grabbed his arm before he started to walk away. "Thanks again."

She nibbled on her nail as her thoughts crashed together inside. How could she not have seen this before? How could her focus have been so narrow? How would things have been different if she hadn't been so stubborn and prideful when Christopher had broken up with her? If she'd actually told him she was pregnant?

But if she'd told him she was pregnant, would he still have made the world a better place?

God's timing was perfect. Maybe this really would all work together for good.

But the time when she was able to speak to Christopher wouldn't come soon enough. All of these years…certainly she could wait another hour or two.

Denton wandered back over to the line of law-enforcement personnel who served as the second line of defense. Her heart beat so fast it seemed to stutter a few beats while trying to keep up. The truth had never seemed clearer before.

"Hey, there," someone said beside her.

She looked up and saw Wally. "I heard about Tech-Share. They called you in, too, huh? I'm surprised they didn't call in the army."

He nodded. "Yeah, they'd called in almost everyone for this one."

"You think it's a setup?"

He shrugged. "You never know. You've got to be careful, though."

"I just hope it's all over soon. I want my old life back."

Her old life back, only with Christopher this time.

"You might have to wait on that for a while."

"What do you mean—?" She looked down and saw the gun protruding from his jacket. Her second moment of truth for the day hit her.

Wally was the one working for the other side, not her brother.

Wally.

She knew her brother couldn't work for people who hated this country. She'd known he was better than that. Thank goodness he was better than that.

But right now, a gun was aimed right at her.

# EIGHTEEN

Christopher took a step back from the house as the SWAT team entered. A winter wind whipped around, its bitter chill almost feeling like an ominous hint of the future.

His gut churned. Something was wrong. He felt sure of it.

Was this a setup? Exactly what was going on here? What was that nagging feeling that told him he was missing something?

He glanced back, expecting to see Ashley standing there in the distance, leaning against the car and watching them just as she'd been doing since they arrived. Staying back a safe distance. Away from harm. Away from danger.

He blinked.

Ashley was gone.

But where?

All of his senses went on alert. Any doubt that something was off disappeared, replaced with complete clarity. Ashley was in trouble, and he had to do something about it. Now.

He jogged back toward the line of police officers and found Denton. "Where's Ashley?"

"She's right over…" He turned and looked over his shoulder. "She was right there."

Christopher kept jogging. He reached the road just in time to see a car pulling away, two heads bobbing inside. He instantly recognized the sedan.

Wally. Wally had Ashley. Wally was one of the bad guys.

He burst into a sprint until he reached his SUV. He threw himself inside, shoved the keys in the ignition and jammed the gears into Drive. Then his foot hit the accelerator. No way was he letting that car out of his sight.

No, the woman he loved was inside. Despite all of the ups and downs of their relationship, their love was the real thing. They'd both made mistakes, both had regrets, but the fact that their paths had led back to each other was no coincidence. This was their second chance and he wasn't going to let it slip away.

Wally's car remained in the distance. Christopher wanted to stay close, but not enough to alert Wally that he was being followed. He had to make sure his timing was flawless—otherwise he might lose them. Tension stretched across his shoulders at the thought.

His phone rang, and he grabbed it out of his pocket. It was Denton.

"Which way are you headed?"

Christopher told him his approximate coordinates.

"Keep me updated. I'm sending backup."

"Just make sure they stay a safe distance behind. I don't want to clue them in that we're on to them," Christopher muttered. Wally merged onto the interstate ahead. Good, it would be easier to remain concealed in the flow of traffic there.

"You know it."

A loud blast filled the phone line. "Denton? What was that? Are you okay?"

Yells and screams sounded in his ear. He could hear

Denton shouting orders to people before coming back on the line. "The house just exploded."

"It exploded?" His muscles stiffened harder.

"Yeah, the whole place was wired. As soon as the door opened, it went up in flames."

"So it was just a trap…" He should have known. These guys had been one—if not more—steps ahead of them this whole time. But that was going to change, and soon.

"Someone knew that email would get Ashley out here. We've been playing their game."

The car ahead of him weaved in and out of traffic. Christopher stayed a safe distance behind them. His heartbeat fast but steady. He wasn't going to let someone else down. He'd had to carry the body of his best friend from the battlefield. He refused to do the same for the woman he loved.

Finally, the sedan pulled off the interstate. It merged into highway traffic and through side streets, remaining in a heavily populated area. Best Christopher could tell, Wally didn't suspect he was being followed.

The sedan finally pulled to a stop in front of a business park. Christopher looked at the sign atop the building… Koury Pharmaceuticals?

The company Ashley had worked for, designing their website? This must be their U.S. production facility.

A car door opened and, a moment later, Wally began dragging Ashley toward the building. The man looked around, as if searching for any onlookers. He never looked Christopher's way, though. Christopher stayed where he was, hidden behind some cars in an adjacent parking lot.

Christopher wanted to jump out and stop him, but he knew the distance between them was too great. He'd have to wait until they got inside, and then pray that he could get inside also. He had to plan his moves carefully. Darkness had fallen, and the blackness would work to his advantage.

He called Denton and let him know where he was. Then he approached the building, searching for security cameras that might clue someone in that he was here. He spotted one at the corner of the building. He had to be fast.

He darted toward the front door. A quick tug told him it was locked. Of course. That didn't surprise him. He pressed himself against the side of the building, hoping that the cameras wouldn't pick up on him there.

He crept around the perimeter of the facility, looking for a crack—a place where he might gain entry. All of the windows were locked, as was a service door in the back. He leaned against the rough bricks, desperate to think of a plan B.

Voices drifted outside. They were muted and impossible to understand. But they were close—on the other side of the window, he guessed.

Slowly, he raised himself up. Blinds covered the glass, but in between the slats he could see inside. Ashley. His heart raced at the sight of her.

She sat at a computer with a gun to her head. Wally stood on one side of her and Gil Travis on the other. Another man—this one with white, thinning hair and a designer business suit on, stood behind them. The man's hands were on his hips as he watched everything unfold, almost appearing like a king looking over his domain.

Everything began to click in his mind.

The unseen head honcho and financial backer behind His People was the president of Koury Pharmaceuticals, wasn't he? He would have the money to fund all of their crazy schemes. And he was influential enough that he'd want to keep his affiliation quiet. If word leaked to the public, his stocks would drop. His company—and the

money he was funneling into the terrorist organization—
would be destroyed. If Christopher remembered correctly,
the pharmaceutical company's headquarters was over in
France. And based on the man's olive complexion, he was
probably from the Middle East.

Christopher glanced to the other side of the room.

His heart lurched when he spotted a little boy beside
Josh in the corner. That had to be David. Now that he
knew who David really was, he couldn't miss how much
the boy looked just like a perfect mix of him and Ashley.

And that boy didn't look like he was scared. He looked
ticked, for that matter. Josh had a hand on his arm, as if
he had to hold the boy back from running over to help
Ashley. Christopher smiled. The boy had a fighting spirit.
Just like he did.

Yes, that night so many years ago was a mistake. But
this little boy wasn't, and Christopher couldn't wait to get
to know him.

But first he had to get inside and save him. And Ashley. More than anything, he wanted to finish their earlier
conversation. He wanted to find out if they ever had another chance together.

Good memories.

That's what he'd make with Ashley and David. That's
what he needed to drive away all of the bad memories that
wanted to haunt him. They'd be better than any therapy.

For the first time in a long time, he felt his first touch
of hope.

An emergency exit door was only a few windows down.

An idea grew in his mind.

He went to the woods and found a rock. He threw it at
the window, then pressed himself into the building on the
other side of the exit door.

Shouts sounded from inside. He drew his gun. He'd

fought for his country for long enough. Now it was time to fight for his family.

As soon as the door opened, he brought the butt of his gun down on the man's head. He sank to the ground. Christopher grabbed the man's gun, stuck it in his waistband and crept inside.

The hallway was clear.

He darted into an empty room. He looked around. A supply closet. At least this would give him a chance to gather his bearings. He couldn't exactly walk into the other room and shoot Wally and Erol Koury in front of David.

No, he needed a plan. And fast.

"Give us the information!" Wally growled.

Ashley's fingers were unsteady on the keyboard. All she could feel was the gun at her temple. All she could think about was how one slip of the finger could end her life—right in front of her son. Sweat sprinkled her forehead, yet her throat remained amazingly dry and sore. "I don't know what you're talking about!"

His other hand pinched her neck. "There are codes embedded into your websites. I need them."

"I didn't put any codes there." Her voice rose in pitch with each word.

Gil Travis—she recognized him from the picture—sneered from the other side. "No, but your brother did."

She craned her neck around. "Josh?"

He shrugged on the floor across the room. He looked pale and tired. But he was alive. So was David. "I had to hide them somewhere. I set up the firewall for you so hackers couldn't get into your sites, but you set up the passcodes."

Yes, she had. They involved several layers of security. Her clients trusted her with their companies' reputations.

She tried to be as careful as possible. Wally pinched at her neck again until she cried out.

"Don't hurt her!" David tried to leap to his feet, but Josh pulled him back down.

She held up a hand. "I'm fine, honey. Don't worry about me."

The boy's eyes held pure determination—just like his father's did. Her heart was comforted, but only for a moment, when she realized he wasn't scared. He was ready to fight.

She looked back over at Erol Koury, the president of Koury Pharmaceuticals. She had no idea he was involved with all of this. But now she understood why he'd hired her—not just for her web expertise but as another way of having a connection with her brother. Nothing was a coincidence when it came to these men.

Wally squeezed her neck again until she gasped with pain. "I don't have any of those codes with me," she insisted.

Erol stormed toward her. "What do you mean you don't have them with you? You don't have them online anywhere?"

She looked up and shook her head. "That wouldn't be very secure, and I promised my clients only the best."

Erol's eyes looked empty as he stared at her, his nostrils flaring. "Where are they, then?"

"They're in my condo, at the bottom of a vase, where hackers can't get to them." After the words tumbled out, she licked her lips, wondering how the men would react.

"At the bottom of a vase?" Erol screamed.

She shrugged. "I figured no one could find them there. I was right. You didn't find them, did you? Even my brilliant brother didn't think to look there."

Erol sighed and ran a hand down his face. "We've

worked too hard to get to this point to let everything fall apart now. None of this was supposed to happen." He swiveled toward Josh. "All you had to do was come work for me, Josh. But no, you had to stand on your principles."

"I love my country more than I love a big paycheck, Erol. Unlike some people." Josh glared at Wally.

Wally narrowed his eyes. "If you had just cooperated, we wouldn't be in this mess right now."

"If you had just had integrity, then so many people wouldn't be dead!" Josh snarled back.

"Quiet! All of you!" Erol paced the room. "Leave the boy here with his dad. Take her and go back to her apartment. Get those passcodes. Now."

As Wally jerked her to her feet, she looked back at Josh. "What kind of codes are embedded on my sites?"

He frowned. "Codes that can destroy the entire infrastructure of the United States—on all levels. Economic, national security...nuclear."

Erol chuckled. "Wouldn't that teach this haughty country not to be so arrogant?"

Wally tried to push her forward, but she dug her heels in and turned back toward her brother again. "Josh, why would you have those kind of codes? I don't understand."

"I had to develop them as a part of my work. Wally worked on the project with me, but my gut told me he wasn't who he claimed." Josh scowled at his former co-worker. "I knew I had to hide the technology I'd developed before the wrong person got their hands on it."

"Why my website?"

"Because I knew they'd be unreachable. You know what I always say. Have layers of security to get through. You were one of my layers. I'm sorry."

Wally jerked her toward the door again. "Come on.

We've got another trip to make. We've got to hurry before you little boyfriend finds us. He's been a real pain."

She glanced back at David. She didn't want to leave him again. But would this buy her more time? More time so that people—that Christopher—could find them? She could only pray that would be the case.

Gun still in hand, Christopher cracked the door open. Two guards stood outside of the office where Ashley was. He'd have to take them down. He could only guess how many other people might be around. When would Denton and his men be here?

He needed backup.

But he might not have time for backup.

He heard the door open, and his back muscles went rigid.

Ashley tumbled out, Wally right behind her. A gun dug into her back. Tears rushed down her cheeks, and her lip bled as if she'd been punched. Anger surged through him.

There was no time to lose, he realized. If he was going to act, it had to be now.

In the shadows of the supply closet, he raised his gun.

Images of his last night in Afghanistan tried to flash back, but he refused to let the memories come. Not now. He couldn't afford to relive the past, not when the future was on the line. He'd saved a country from a terrorist. Certainly he could save the woman he loved.

With the precision of the sharpshooter he'd been, he aimed at Wally. He waited, making sure no one else stepped out behind them. The door closed, and Wally shoved Ashley again.

That's when Christopher pulled the trigger.

Wally went down, moaning in pain. The guards flanking him scrambled in a panic. In the mad flurry of activity, he didn't have a clean shot.

"Right there!" One of the guards spotted him and raised his gun.

Christopher shot the man's shoulder. Quickly, he got the other guard in his crosshairs and fired. He went down with a cry. He hadn't shot to kill, only to maim.

Ashley's eyes widened as she looked down the hallway. Was there someone else? Someone he couldn't see because of the door beside him?

Ashley reached behind her and pulled out her own gun. She'd brought her gun, just like he encouraged her to do. Good girl.

With trembling hands, she pressed the trigger. Christopher heard a grunt outside his door and the crash of someone hitting the floor. Ashley may have just saved his life.

Ashley waved him over, her head swerving from side to side as she checked to see if the coast was clear. He pushed open the door and ran toward her, knowing that they didn't have much time before more men came running. He grabbed the guards' guns and dropped them in a trash can out of their reach.

His eyes quickly soaked Ashley in when he reached her. She appeared shaken but otherwise fine. "You okay?"

She nodded, gratitude filling her gaze. "Better now that you're here."

Christopher reached for the door. They had to get David and Josh. Now.

Just as they stepped in, Erol had David in a chokehold. "Not so fast," he muttered. "You're not as smart as you think you are. Put down your guns or the boy gets hurt."

"No one needs to get hurt," Christopher muttered. His eyes were on David. His son. His sweet son. The boy's perceptive gaze flickered from Ashley to Christopher, keen intelligence flashing in his eyes.

"Put your guns down," Erol ordered.

Christopher began lowering his gun to the floor when David suddenly bit Erol's arm. The man howled with pain.

It was just the break they needed. Christopher swooped up his gun again. In three quick strokes, he'd pulled David away from Erol, kicked the gun out of his hand, and snapped the man's arms behind him.

Lights flashed outside. Feet trampled close by. Shouts ensued.

Help was here.

They were safe.

Finally, they were safe.

After everyone had been successfully taken into custody and as the feds scurried about the building collecting evidence, Christopher squatted down next to David. His son. His heart stuttered at the mere thought of it. As he glanced in the boy's eyes for the first time, an indescribable love filled him.

*Take it easy, Jordan,* he reminded himself. *That boy has no idea who you are.*

He smiled, trying to look more relaxed than he felt. "That was an awfully brave thing you did there."

The boy raised his chin—just like Ashley always did. He had Ashley's oval face and chin, but his hair and eye color. Pure determination filled his gaze. "I don't like to see people bullied. It's not right."

Christopher grinned. He already liked David, and he couldn't wait to get to know him better. He still had so much to learn, so much he'd like to teach him—if Ashley and Josh would let him be a part of the boy's life. They hadn't gotten that far in their conversations. But he hoped to be a part of Ashley's life also. He glanced over at her, saw how much she loved the boy, and he suddenly understood why she wanted to protect him so much. It didn't justify what she'd done, but he knew forgiveness was a powerful tool and one that he was more than willing to employ right now.

For the sake of his family. Hope like he hadn't felt in a long time filled him.

Ashley hadn't stopped hugging David since Erol had been apprehended. Josh had been led away to be debriefed. But he paused for long enough to mutter a "thank you" and "sorry."

Ashley pulled away from David and looked at the boy, her eyes full of warmth. She looked beautiful, even with blood trickling down her forehead and the start of a bruise at the side of her eye.

She glanced at Christopher and sucked in a deep breath. "David, this is my friend, Christopher. He's been looking forward to meeting you."

Christopher continued to soak in the boy in front of him. He looked like he'd been well taken care of, even in his captivity. Even if he hadn't been, Christopher had a feeling that the boy wasn't the type to be a victim. He was the type to stay strong and resilient. "You're a little trouper, just like your aunt said."

Their eyes met, and Ashley smiled before muttering, "The apple doesn't fall far from the tree."

David's voice cut into their moment, the time when unspoken promises were made, but no one knew except the two of them. "What does that mean? Who has apples?"

"I'll explain later." She studied his face. "Are you okay? Are you really okay? I was worried about you."

He shrugged and pushed out his lips as if bored. "I guess. I missed you, Ashley."

Ashley's arms seemed to squeeze him tighter. "I missed you, too. More than you can ever know."

"I want to build a snowman with you. Those men wouldn't let me go outside and play. They weren't very nice, but they did feed me cheese puffs. Lots and lots of cheese puffs."

Christopher smiled this time. "I'm sure we can arrange something, as soon as we're cleared to leave here."

"You know what tomorrow is?" David's eyes lit with excitement. He didn't let them answer. "It's Christmas Eve!"

Christopher and Ashley shared another glance. He'd all but forgotten just how close the holiday was. With everything else that had been going on, they'd all been a little distracted.

David frowned. "My dad said he probably wasn't going to be able to spend it with me. He said he might have to go away for a while, but that I could stay with you, Ashley."

Ashley squeezed his arm. "You're always welcome to stay with me."

"He told me your secret." David's eyes glowed as he stared up at her.

Ashley's face went white. "What secret?"

"He told me that you're my mom."

Ashley blinked, as if uncertain whether or not to believe him. "He…he told you that?"

"It's okay, Ashley. You've always been like my mom. I think Dad was afraid something would happen to him. He said I'd never be alone, that my family was bigger than I realized."

Ashley looked up at Christopher, bewilderment across her features. They needed to talk. There was so much they needed to discuss. He could see it in Ashley's eyes that she felt the same way about him as Christopher did about her.

Medics rushed into the room. "We need to check you all over for injuries," one of them said.

They'd have to put off a conversation they should have had nearly a decade ago. But this time he wasn't going to let Ashley slip away from him again.

They reached another safe house, this one a cozy bungalow located on a lake in the foothills of the Blue Ridge Mountains. Ashley had helped David get ready for bed, read him a bedtime story, and then tucked him into bed.

Her throat ached as she walked into the living room. Christopher stoked the fire. He rose to his feet when he spotted her.

She rubbed her hands on her jeans. They'd had a lot of tough conversations already. But this one required not only owning up to the past but presenting an offer for the future.

She hooked a hair behind her ear as she reached him. "Can I talk to you a minute, Christopher?"

His gaze was steady on hers…steady and warm. "Of course."

A shiver raced through her when she heard the huskiness in his voice. She pointed to the couch. "We should sit."

They sat across from each other, close enough that their knees touched.

She rubbed her hands on her jeans again as her gaze reached up to meet his. "Look, I know we've been through a lot. I know you're angry with me, and I deserve it. I should have pushed through my emotions and realized that telling you about David was the right thing. Sometimes it's easier to realize these things in retrospect."

"That's true for all of us, Ashley."

She rested her hand on his knee. "I just wanted to say that I understand. Finally. I talked to Denton and after our conversation it just clicked in my mind, and I understand now why you had to go to Afghanistan."

"You do?" Light gleamed in his eyes.

She nodded, her emotions squeezing her. "I feel like I was actually the one being selfish throughout the whole thing. I can see that now."

His hand covered hers. "That's not true. It was an agonizing decision, no matter how you looked at it. There were no real winners."

"Except maybe the world." She offered a small smile.

Christopher gave her one in return. It quickly disappeared, replaced with a firm-set jaw and serious eyes. "I'd like to think the world is a better place, that my sacrifices weren't for nothing."

"No, the world is a better place."

He scooted closer. "I wish you didn't have to get hurt in the process." He cupped her cheek with one hand. "Ashley, you've always been the only one for me. No one else has even remotely caught my eye. My heart's always been with you."

Her spirit seemed to breathe with new life, lifting with hope inside her. "Even as mad as I was, I've always loved you, Christopher. Always."

His other arm snaked around her waist and he pulled her close. Their lips met, sweetly, tenderly.

After the heartbreak of the past week, Ashley realized one thing: all things do work together for the good of those who love Christ. Sometimes it just might take years to realize it, though.

# EPILOGUE

Ashley straightened the white slacks and snow-white sweater she wore. It wasn't exactly a wedding dress, but there would be time for a big wedding later—if that's what she and Christopher decided on. Really, the wedding was so unimportant to her. It was the marriage that mattered.

Instead of planning and waiting for a future date, she and Christopher had decided to get married in a small ceremony at the Eyes' headquarters. They'd had eight long years of being apart. Neither wanted to waste any more time.

In five minutes, it would be the New Year and they would officially become husband and wife. Mr. and Mrs. Christopher Jordan. It had a nice ring to it. It always had.

She stood before a chaplain with a small audience gathered around her in the massive lobby area at Eyes. David was at her side, holding their rings, and looking handsome in some khakis, an olive-green sweater and a Navy ball cap that Christopher had given him. The boy hadn't wanted to take it off.

The two of them bonded quickly, and David already looked up at Christopher with a glimmer of admiration in his eyes. Christopher had told his son stories—happy, adventurous ones—about being a SEAL, about training, about toughening up. David held on to each word and asked questions. They'd talked about fishing and hiking and playing football.

Josh, in the meantime, had been sent into hiding for a while, at least until some of this storm passed. He knew too much, had seen too much. He'd asked Ashley and Christopher if they'd watch out for David. He'd told them he'd had moments of clarity while in captivity, and that's why he'd told David that Ashley was really his mom. David had taken it all in stride, something that Ashley was immensely thankful for.

They hadn't yet told him that Christopher was his real daddy, but they would with time. When the right moment came, they'd know it. They didn't want to give the boy too much to handle at once.

Christopher stood in front of her, wearing jeans and a Kelly-green sweater that made his eyes pop. A fire blazed in the background. The Christmas tree stood in the corner still, and some of Christopher's friends—and the very people who'd kept them both alive during this whole ordeal—sat around them.

Ashley hardly saw anyone except for Christopher and David. Her soon-to-be husband squeezed her hands, never taking his eyes off her since the start of the ceremony. She was so glad that their paths had led them back to each other. She praised God for truly working all things together for their good.

"Ashley, do you take this man, Christopher Jordan, to be your lawfully wedded husband?" the chaplain asked. "To have and to hold from this day forward."

Ashley's heart glowed with warmth as she looked up at Christopher. This was the moment she'd been dreaming about for so long. It almost seemed surreal, as if she'd wake up and he'd be gone. He squeezed her hands again, as if reading her thoughts, and reminding her that this was no dream.

She smiled. "I do."

"Christopher, do you take this woman, Ashley Wilson, to be your lawfully wedded wife?"

"You better believe it." The look in his eyes was pure affection, unmasked and unbridled and out there for everyone to see.

"I now pronounce you man and wife. You may—" the chaplain glanced at his watch and paused for a second before looking up with a grin "—kiss the bride."

Just as Christopher's lips came down on hers, balloons and confetti rained down on them from above.

"Happy New Year!" everyone around them yelled.

Laughing, they stepped back. Ashley put her arm around David's shoulders and pulled him into a group hug with Christopher as everyone cheered.

Her family. Together at last.

It truly was going to be a happy new year.

A happy lifetime for that matter, as long as Christopher and David were by her side.

* * * * *

Dear Reader,

As I was listening to a radio interview with a former Navy SEAL not long ago, I found myself fascinated with what he had to say. He talked about how hard it was to be a Navy SEAL and to have a family, saying that it was extremely difficult to be committed to both.

That interview made me start thinking about the sacrifices our military personnel make, especially those who are in the Special Forces. Long deployments, stress from the battlefield and trouble adjusting to life back at home are only a few of the challenges these families face. Not long after listening to that interview, this book was born.

I hope you enjoyed Ashley and Christopher's story, along with the reminder that God can work everything—even our mistakes—together for our good.

## Questions for Discussion

1. Ashley likes having a certain amount of control in her life, but she finds everything spiraling out of control at the start of this book. What do you do when life starts going in a different direction than you originally planned? Do you act in faith or fear?

2. Ashley and Christopher both have traumatic things that have happened in their past that affect them today. Do you have anything like this in your life? How did you overcome it?

3. Ashley regrets her decision not to tell Christopher about David. Each of us lives with regrets—some big, some small. How can we put regrets into perspective?

4. What's your biggest regret? How have you learned from it? Is there anything you can do to make things right?

5. Ashley let a fair amount of bitterness build up after her breakup with Christopher, and she even let it cloud her judgment on more than one occasion. Have you ever had a time in your life when bitterness overcame you? How did you heal from the emotion?

6. What causes bitterness to form in our lives? How can we avoid it?

7. Ashley has a breakthrough moment about Christopher after she talks to Denton. Have you had any breakthrough moments where you gained new perspective?

8. Sometimes a new perspective can be a game changer. Sometimes it can be as simple as trying to view someone else through God's eyes instead of our own, or operating on the "glass half full" notion. Are there any "perspectives" you need to change in your daily life?

9. John 14:27 says, *Peace I leave with you; my peace I give to you. Not as the world gives do I give to you. Let not your hearts be troubled, neither let them be afraid.* Do you struggle with a troubled, fearful heart?

10. What are some simple steps we can take to overcome the obstacles in our lives that keep us from living fully? How can we be surrounded by God's peace?

COMING NEXT MONTH FROM
**Love Inspired® Suspense**

Available December 3, 2013

## CHRISTMAS COVER-UP
*Family Reunions*
by Lynette Eason

For fourteen years, Detective Kate Randall has never stopped looking for her sister. The closer she and former FBI special agent Jordan Grey get to answers, the more desperate—and deadly—the kidnapper becomes.

## FORCE OF NATURE
*Stormswept*
by Dana Mentink

Caught in the midst of a hurricane and a dangerous drug-trafficking ring, Antonia Verde's only chance of survival is the man who once broke her heart.

## YULETIDE JEOPARDY
*The Cold Case Files*
by Sandra Robbins

When new clues emerge about a decade-old case, can police detective Alex Crowne look past his feelings for anchorwoman Grace Kincaid before his ex-fiancée becomes a killer's newest victim?

## WILDERNESS PERIL
by Elizabeth Goddard

Stranded in the Alaskan bush, a routine repossession turns sour when pilot Rick Savage and mechanic Shay Ridiker are taken prisoner by a nefarious gold mining operation!

---

# REQUEST YOUR FREE BOOKS!
## 2 FREE RIVETING INSPIRATIONAL NOVELS
## PLUS 2 FREE MYSTERY GIFTS

**YES!** Please send me 2 FREE Love Inspired® Suspense novels and my 2 FREE mystery gifts (gifts are worth about $10). After receiving them, if I don't wish to receive any more books, I can return the shipping statement marked "cancel." If I don't cancel, I will receive 4 brand-new novels every month and be billed just $4.74 per book in the U.S. or $5.24 per book in Canada. That's a savings of at least 21% off the cover price. It's quite a bargain! Shipping and handling is just 50¢ per book in the U.S. and 75¢ per book in Canada.* I understand that accepting the 2 free books and gifts places me under no obligation to buy anything. I can always return a shipment and cancel at any time. Even if I never buy another book, the two free books and gifts are mine to keep forever.

123/323 IDN F5AC

Name _____ (PLEASE PRINT) _____

Address _____ Apt. # _____

City _____ State/Prov. _____ Zip/Postal Code _____

Signature (if under 18, a parent or guardian must sign) _____

### Mail to the **Harlequin® Reader Service:**
**IN U.S.A.:** P.O. Box 1867, Buffalo, NY 14240-1867
**IN CANADA:** P.O. Box 609, Fort Erie, Ontario L2A 5X3

**Are you a current subscriber to Love Inspired Suspense books
and want to receive the larger-print edition?
Call 1-800-873-8635 or visit www.ReaderService.com.**

* Terms and prices subject to change without notice. Prices do not include applicable taxes. Sales tax applicable in N.Y. Canadian residents will be charged applicable taxes. Offer not valid in Quebec. This offer is limited to one order per household. Not valid for current subscribers to Love Inspired Suspense books. All orders subject to credit approval. Credit or debit balances in a customer's account(s) may be offset by any other outstanding balance owed by or to the customer. Please allow 4 to 6 weeks for delivery. Offer available while quantities last.

**Your Privacy**—The Harlequin® Reader Service is committed to protecting your privacy. Our Privacy Policy is available online at www.ReaderService.com or upon request from the Harlequin Reader Service.
We make a portion of our mailing list available to reputable third parties that offer products we believe may interest you. If you prefer that we not exchange your name with third parties, or if you wish to clarify or modify your communication preferences, please visit us at www.ReaderService.com/consumerschoice or write to us at Harlequin Reader Service Preference Service, P.O. Box 9062, Buffalo, NY 14269. Include your complete name and address.

LIS13R

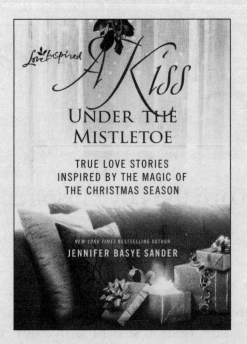

Christmas has a way of reminding us of what really matters—and what could be more important than our loved ones? From husbands and wives to boyfriends and girlfriends to long-lost loves, the real-life romances in this book are surrounded by the joy and blessings of the Christmas season.

Featuring stories by favorite Love Inspired authors, this collection will warm your heart and soothe your soul through the long winter. *A Kiss Under the Mistletoe* beautifully celebrates the way love and faith can transform a cold day in December into the most magical day of the year.

**On sale now!**

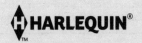

HNAKUTM11

# Love the Love Inspired book you just read?

### Your opinion matters.

**Review this book on your favorite book site, review site, blog or your own social media properties and share your opinion with other readers!**

**Be sure to connect with us at:**
Harlequin.com/Newsletters
Twitter.com/LoveInspiredBks
Facebook.com/LoveInspiredBooks